ALSO BY PALMER JONES

HER IRISH CHEF

O'KEELEY'S IRISH PUB- BOOK TWO

PALMER JONES

Print Edition: 978-1-7333968-3-7

E-Book Edition: 978-1-7333968-2-0

Cover design by JD&J Design.

Editing by Patricia Ogilvie.

First Edition

For M&A

1

He was screwed.

Rian O'Keeley pushed through the crowd at the Atlanta airport, heading toward the parking deck. A week in California did not inspire a new dish for the restaurant he shared with his brothers. Instead, he came home to a shitty review from a food critic and his version of writer's block.

He unlocked his sleek Mercedes, sat down, and slammed the door shut harder than necessary. Damn it. The interview he just gave to one of the top food magazines in the world included a bold declaration that a new fusion, something to combine his Irish upbringing with his new home in America, would be on the menu at O'Keeley's by the end of the year. And, so far, he didn't have a single, damn idea.

Years spent traveling around the world had been a waste of time to get to this point in his career and choke. And it wasn't just his name on the line.

The drive to O'Keeley's Irish Pub gave him plenty of time to cool off before seeing his family. He was the level-headed brother of the three. Or at least he'd assumed that role by default. Someone had to play the part of the peacekeeper with an overbearing brother like Brogan and a feckless younger brother, Cathal.

He pulled into the employee parking lot in downtown Atlanta, parking beside Brogan's four-door sedan. His oldest brother also held the title for being the most responsible. He ran the day-to-day operations of the pub. And it was because of Brogan's new wife, Selena, that Rian found himself back in Atlanta instead of traveling to another part of the United States looking for inspiration.

He rose from the car, the Georgia heat and humidity closing in around him. He'd never get used to it.

Selena waited at the front entrance, arms crossed, toe tapping, her golden hair pulled back. "You were supposed to call when you left the airport."

He paused beside his sister-in-law, planted a kiss on top of her head, and then headed toward the kitchen. "Why? I already knew you'd track the flight." He wiggled his phone in her direction. "I'm surprised you aren't tracking me by now."

She took two steps to his one to keep up. "That's because you don't communicate. We arranged for the kids from the community center to visit today. *Your* idea, by the way."

Yes, it had been his idea. That was before his future looked shot to hell by his lack of creativity.

"The kids will be here any minute, Rian."

"I know." He pushed open the kitchen doors and let the feeling of coming home take away his stress. He loved working in O'Keeley's. It smelled clean along with just a hint of Irish stew they'd made the night before. He'd designed the kitchen himself. The counters were a little higher than average to accommodate his height. Bright lights. Wide spaces between workstations.

It took up more area than most kitchens in a restaurant. Typically, the main floor with additional seating was a priority. Rian held a third of the ownership in the restaurant. He had a third of the decision-making power.

"Selena—" Brogan paused as he pushed open the door. "Oh. Good. You're here. The kids just arrived."

Rian shot Selena a bright smile. "All that stress for nothing. I'm obviously on time then."

Selena rolled her eyes. "You're killing me."

"That's what brothers do." He grinned and winked at her, finally getting a smile.

"You and Cathal think you can get away with anything by flirting."

Rian leaned over, his arms resting on the cold, stainless steel counter. "And, my dear, how does your husband get away with things? Does Brogan flirt with you as well?"

Selena laughed. "I'm not sure you want the details to that." She pushed open the door.

The sound of voices drifted in a moment before becoming muffled again as the door closed.

Nonstop chatter, to be exact. The cooking demonstration would teach the kids both the tools to make healthy food choices and give them a glimpse of his career.

Rian laid out the ingredients. Selena stuck her head into the kitchen. "Are you almost ready?" She straightened and pointed to the zucchini. "You do realize these are kids?" she asked.

"Yes. Kids should eat vegetables."

"French fries and macaroni and cheese are vegetables at this age." She laughed when he made a face. "Not everyone grew up with a freaking garden in the backyard of their cottage in Ireland."

Maybe not, but he'd try to expose them while he had the chance.

"I'll bring them back." She turned to leave then stopped, her golden eyes settling on him. "Try not to be so quiet."

"I have to talk, Selena. I'm giving a cooking demonstration."

"Yes, I know, but you have such a great personality." She stepped back to him and gave him a quick kiss on the cheek. "You should let that come out a little quicker."

He crossed his arms. "I feel like you're trying to tell me that people don't like me."

"Eh," she murmured, waving her hand side to side. "You can come across as aloof."

"Maybe I'm aloof when I'm not in the mood to talk."

Selena huffed. "You're impossible." She left him alone. He smiled. He'd have never thought his older brother would have ever found a woman to actually marry his grumpy ass, but there she went, the newest member of the O'Keeley clan.

Just as bossy as Brogan.

And having close friends wasn't an issue for Rian. It was rare for him to call someone a close friend, but they existed. He gave so much of himself conducting interviews or cooking around the world, that when he was home, he wanted to live quietly.

The children's chatter drew closer. He took a deep breath as they walked in through the kitchen door.

The voices rose even higher, if possible, all talking at once – a blur of faces.

Rian blinked, trying to sort it out and questioning his sanity for doing this.

A woman brought up the rear of the group, her lips moving fast and giving out directions. She kept her face averted, quieting them down as she passed by them until she stopped in front of Rian.

Her heart-shaped face and guarded smile fascinated him – warm brown eyes with full lips. No makeup. The only thing he could think to say was, "hi," as he held out his hand.

Her smile faltered. For some strange reason, he wanted to make her smile.

She shook his hand, her eyes locked on their hands. "I'm Mara Andrews."

"Rian O'Keeley." Her hand felt cool, her skin a beautiful contrast to his own.

Selena cleared her throat. "Rian?"

He reluctantly dropped Mara's hand. "Sorry. Kids. Right." He scanned his audience. Most of them were under sixteen. A little girl stood in the front, her eyes wide.

"Hi, there," he said.

She tilted her head back. "You're tall."

He chuckled. "You're short."

She grinned, missing two teeth. "My name is Blair."

He spoke in French. "You have a very pretty dress, Blair."

Her eyes sparkled. "What did you say?"

"He said you have a very pretty dress." Mara's smile appeared a little more genuine.

"You speak French?" That surprised and pleased him.

"Yes. I lived there for a year when I was in college."

If her face hadn't captivated him, that small fact did. He spent most of his time in Europe and mostly in France. He opened his mouth to ask her where.

Selena's sharp elbow caught him in his ribs. "You're acting no better than Cathal," she mumbled.

That comparison grabbed his attention. His younger brother's hobby would be classified as picking up women.

And he was damned good at it, too. But Rian had an audience of kids watching his every move. Convincing their chaperon to go on a date would have to wait.

But if she were available, it would happen.

"Let's get started," Rian said. "We've set out a workstation for each of you. We'll start with peeling zucchini and cracking eggs." Selena and Mara organized the kids, placing one at each station.

He watched Mara, openly, so he noticed each time she glanced in his direction.

She settled in beside Blair, laughing each time the little girl cracked an egg. The director seemed happy. He liked that. He'd dated women from all walks of life, all ethnicities, all races. Happiness was the number one trait that he liked when thinking of going out on a date.

He'd had enough sadness and frustration in the past.

Selena moved through the older kids peeling zucchini. She was a natural with children. Not that it surprised him, but it reassured him that at least his brother's wife might have an idea what she was doing should they start a family soon. In his opinion, Brogan was a lost cause. The man would probably buy a suit for his son or daughter before they turned one.

"Mr. O'Keeley?" Mara shifted from behind the counter. She bit her lower lip. "Or Chef? I'm not sure what to call you."

"The title of Mr. O'Keeley belongs to my older brother." He wiped his hands on the towel hanging from his back pocket. "Rian is fine."

"Rian," she said, causing him to want to hear it again. Her Southern accent was soft, dragging out the first vowel in his name in a cute way.

"I like your accent."

She laughed. "Mine? You're the one with the major accent in the room." She pushed a piece of hair behind her ear. "I was wondering if you'd consider doing this again. Maybe teaching them a dish they can make at home. Out of easy ingredients? I'd purchase the food, but I can already tell the kids, especially the boys, are completely impressed by you. That doesn't happen often. We have a small kitchen in the after-school center you could use."

Her eyes held his, and he knew he should give her an answer. But it wasn't one he wished he could give her. "My schedule is fairly busy."

Her gaze dropped. "Oh. I knew it might be. It was just a suggestion."

"Wait." He pulled his phone from his pocket. "When were you thinking?"

"Anytime." She chewed on her bottom lip again.

He cleared his throat. "I'm free on Friday."

Selena slapped a hand down on the countertop, causing an egg to roll to the edge. She caught it and shook it at him. "Seriously, Rian. Cathal is definitely rubbing off on you, picking up women whenever you get the chance."

Rian set his phone down, giving Selena a sharp look. "I was scheduling when I could come and give them a demonstration at their after-school center, *dear sister.*"

Selena blushed and gave Mara an apologetic look. "Sorry. I'm just trying to help keep him on track. O'Keeley men are easily distracted by pretty women."

Rian shook his head. "I won't deny that statement. I'm more concerned about your mental health, seeing that you picked the surliest one of the three of us."

"Brogan can be very charming when he's not working."

"Which is never." Rian's phone chimed. He wagged it toward Selena. "If you want to help me, then go tell my brother to lay off texting me about next month's specials. He's gotten pushier since he married you. If that was possible. That's the fifth text since yesterday."

She tilted her nose in the air. "I sent the first three from his phone. You stopped answering mine." She turned on her heel and walked over to check on the kids.

He shifted back to Mara, who gave him a small, sympathetic smile. "I'd say sorry, but I'm afraid everyone has to deal with family. Mine's pretty crazy."

"Selena is the best thing that could have happened to my brother Brogan. But when she gets something in her mind, there's no slowing her down." He fired off a text to Selena.

A second later, Selena's head snapped up, eyes narrowing.

He threw his head back and laughed.

"What?" Mara looked between the two of them, seeming to enjoy the byplay.

"She wanted next month's specials for the menu." He held out his phone for Mara to read. She angled closer, a smell of fresh peaches drifted toward him. She smelled like dessert.

She smiled a real, gorgeous smile that lit up her brown eyes. "I don't believe for one second you're going to serve peanut butter and jelly sandwiches."

"I was inspired by the youth of America."

"I could actually afford to come here if you served something like that."

Her comment pushed him back a step. He wanted her to come, enjoy the restaurant. Sit with him. Talk to him. Give him the privilege of watching her eyes dance when she laughed.

"Friday night. After I cook with the kids, you and I will come here for dinner."

Her smile vanished. "Just us?"

"Why not? If you want to eat here, that is. You just mentioned it, so I thought you might like to come with me."

"I'd think you'd be sick of eating your food."

"Coming to O'Keeley's is the closest I usually get to eating my food." He dropped his voice to a whisper, moving closer. A horrible excuse, but he was no better than Cathal as Selena had pointed out to him. "I don't often cook alone."

Her eyes gleamed with amusement, and she imitated his whisper. "I'm guessing you're not alone...often."

That was an odd statement. "What does that mean?"

She lifted a shoulder and glanced away. "I saw the pictures of you on the yacht. I assume you are with people. All of the time."

That couldn't be farther from the truth. He loved being alone. Living alone. Waking up alone. For some men, like Cathal, they hated it. His youngest brother dated woman after woman, treating them over-the-top to make up for his past. Using them as a distraction for a few weeks, or a few hours, and then parting with them. Strangely, he treated them so wonderfully that none of his past dates ever held ill feelings toward him.

Rian's past had the opposite effect. He enjoyed dating, but for him, it was temporary, and second dates were rare. He had no desire ever to have a long-term relationship, so he never formed any real attachment. And usually, he left before the sun rose.

There were too many mad memories lurking in the corners of his mind. A commitment meant a woman wanted every detail of your past.

He wanted those details to remain locked away.

"I can assure you, I'm alone far more often than the

internet gives me credit. The woman in those pictures, the one with the blond hair—"

"And legs for days. Yes. I saw." She drummed her fingers on the counter. "What about her?"

"The owner of the boat's wife. If you had the full picture, you'd see that he was sitting on the other side of her. He's an old friend." He tapped her cell phone. "Don't believe everything you read, Mara."

She searched his face. "Obviously, I shouldn't."

"Friday. I'll drive you from the center here after I work with the kids. You can pick what you call it."

She smirked. "I assumed it's just a dinner. Why? What were you going to call it?"

"What I plan on it being." He moved around the counter, pausing beside her. His arm pressed against her shoulder.

Her eyes widened, but she didn't move or pull away. She wasn't very tall, maybe five-eight. Nothing compared to his six-two height, but her curves, now that he had a clear view of her, confirmed that his physical attraction to her was magnetic.

"It's a date."

2

"Why aren't you married, Ms. Mara? Don't you want to be?"

Nine-year-olds could be so darn cute. And observant. Amara Andrews gave Blair a stiff smile. "Because I haven't found the right man."

She'd almost responded with, "because the man I was going to marry ended up being a jackass," but poor Blair could find out that not everyone was like Prince Charming when she was a little older. She didn't need her dreams crushed at nine.

"I'm going to marry Bruno Mars." She clasped her hands together. "He's hot."

Mara couldn't help but laugh. Blair had no clue what that meant. She repeated everything the older girls said. "I'm sure he's very lucky to have such a smart little girl like you. But I bet even Bruno Mars would want you to know how to subtract double digits. C'mon. Concentrate now so we can earn those M&Ms."

Bribery. Sometimes, it was all inner-city kids responded

to. Learning math because it would help them later, much, much later, was a hard concept for kids like Blair.

"Mara?" The director called from the door of her corner office.

Mara pointed to the next problem. "Work this on your own." She left Blair and walked across the tiled floor of the old warehouse. The after-school program had recently opened up in a new location in downtown Atlanta. It wasn't much to an outsider, but to the kids and staff, it was everything. Plenty of space to play basketball or, as the older kids liked, dodgeball.

She'd sure as hell never offer to play that again. Her boys took no mercy.

"Yes, Mrs. Peterson?" Mara sat down in the one, plastic chair across the desk. The office wasn't much bigger than a bathroom stall, but Mrs. Peterson was entitled to the only office. Her boss was a stern woman, late fifties, with blonde hair that she'd never let go gray.

"The job will officially post next week. I wanted to make sure you were aware of it." She sat down at her desk, giving Mara the same look she sometimes gave the kids in trouble. "I have significant pull with the selection of my replacement. I know you've worked hard, but we both know you have areas you can improve."

"Yes, ma'am." She didn't agree. Mara had watched Mrs. Peterson for the past ten years. She knew exactly how she'd run the program and things she'd change.

And, of course, a pay raise would be nice. She earned enough to get by, alternating between a part-time receptionist and her assistant director position at the after-school program, but she wanted the job. Her degree in psychology and master's in social work had earned her a big student loan and a little paycheck.

As much as she respected her boss, she'd only taken the job in the hopes of running the program one day. It just seemed like that day might never come.

Until now.

Geez, what if she didn't get it?

"Rian O'Keeley is due here soon, correct?"

Rian. Yes, the man with the sexy as hell accent, tousled brown hair, and blue-green hazel eyes that made her heart stop when he'd asked her on a date.

Her.

Men had asked her on dates before, attractive, successful men. But it did something to a girl's soul when someone *that* hot asks her out.

Mrs. Peterson clasped her hands together and set them on the desk. "Mrs. O'Keeley said that the restaurant wanted to do some additional community outreach. She's offered to provide fifty-dollar gift certificates to each child who participates today in the cooking class that Mr. O'Keeley will teach."

"They're going to give a fifty-dollar gift card to each kid? Wow. That's really generous." And she would get dinner at O'Keeley's tonight with Rian. She looked away from Mrs. Peterson, hoping the excitement didn't show. Having a date with a man like him beat going home to her apartment with her cat, Dash, who hated her. Oh, and the frozen Salisbury steak dinner she had waiting in the freezer.

"She said it was Rian's idea."

Mara pulled out her phone, searching for him as she'd done before. There he was, lounging on a yacht. And there was his leggy blonde, in all her perfection.

The woman might only be a friend to Rian, but Mara was still a little jealous. Those were the types of people he socialized with. Not social workers that lived in a studio apartment. The only culinary taste she'd acquired over the years was which brands and entrees she enjoyed for dinner in the frozen food section.

She'd not dated anyone seriously since she'd broken off her engagement to Shane. Luckily, Shane still lived back home in the middle of Alabama. Her stomach tightened the same way it did with the memory of that volatile relationship. For *years* she stayed with him because it was expected of her. She never saw a way out. Her parents, friends, everyone loved him.

She pulled her shoulders back. She'd worked too hard in the past two years to let it affect her any longer. Rian had asked her out. She'd go without bringing her ex and his memories on the date with her.

"Ms. Andrews, I did it!" Blair stood in the doorway and held up her paper. Mara walked over to her. This was her calling, helping children.

"Oh, honey," Mara began, pointing at the first column on the first problem. "Let's do it together."

After working with Blair for another ten minutes, Mara left to go to the grocery store and buy the ingredients for Rian's demonstration. She spotted his sports car near the entrance when she returned, and the situation hit her full force. A strange buzzing ran through her body. Nerves? Probably. Her fingers tightened on the grocery bags.

She stepped into the center as Rian emerged from the kitchen. He was early. And looking delicious. He'd worn tan slacks and a red button-down shirt with the sleeves rolled up, revealing toned forearms.

A date.

With that man. She'd be lucky if she didn't make a fool of herself before the date even began and he found a reason to make other plans. Her kids might have behaved on the field trip to O'Keeley's, but they weren't entirely predictable when they were at the center. That included little Blair.

But contemplating her date would have to wait. Blair's cry echoed throughout the center.

Mara's steps quickened. The little girl's learning disability caused a wave of emotions when she became frustrated. And, judging by the screams coming from Mrs. Peterson's office, Blair was having a moment.

"Sorry." She handed Rian the bag of ingredients, unable to revel in the way his fingers brushed along her wrists. "I need to see to Blair."

"What's wrong?" Instead of going back into the kitchen, he motioned Romeo, one of her students, over and passed off the bag. "Take these to the kitchen."

The teenager, who usually hated every authority figure possible, nodded and walked away. She'd have to figure out Romeo later. She broke into a jog at Blair's next high-pitched scream.

She turned into the office. Blair sat curled into a ball in the plastic chair with her hands over her ears.

The director threw her hands up, her voice shrill. "Maybe she'll respond to you. You left, and she had a meltdown. She's too dependent on you. I've told you that before."

Mara squatted in front of Blair, brushing the hair back from her face. The way Blair coped with the uncertainty of the world was to push it away. She'd curl into the ball, hands over her ears.

She'd worked with her, trying to find other ways for Blair to deal with her frustration when things didn't go her way. Mrs. Peterson lacked the same patience.

Blair jerked when Mara set a hand on her shoulder. Her hand knocked Mara in the face, sending her toppling backward onto her butt, the back of her head hitting Mrs. Peterson's desk. A cup of pens and pencils bounced off her shoulder and scattered on the ground.

Rian's warm hand wrapped around her arm. "Are you alright?"

"Fine." Great. Here was the embarrassing part where Rian realized she wasn't in his league.

"Can I try to help?" He waited for Mara to stand, his hand lingering along her elbow longer than necessary. Not that she'd complain that an amazing looking man like Rian touched her too long. Nope. Those words would never come from her lips.

He leaned over the back of the chair and began whispering in French to Blair. It was *Twinkle, Twinkle Little Star*. Blair tilted her head to the side, cutting her eyes up at him, and he smiled. If Blair actually understood what a *hot* man was, she'd dump her Bruno Mars for Rian. No offense, Bruno.

Mrs. Peterson sighed and stared at Rian like he was her Bruno.

Rian slowed down and said one word at a time, letting Blair repeat them back to him. She sat up and sang the little verse. She pronounced it with reasonable accuracy.

Mara sang the song in her head along with them. She wouldn't break whatever spell he'd cast over Blair to help calm her down.

Rian held his hand out for Blair to hold. "Can you help make our snacks?"

She nodded, and he led her out the door.

Mara paused before following them and looked at Mrs. Peterson. Guilt forced her to mention their date. "I'm having dinner with him tonight. He invited me to O'Keeley's after work." She couldn't hide it. If she did, it meant she had expectations that the dinner was something more than a nice gesture from Rian.

Mrs. Peterson's whimsical look dropped from her face. "You realize we have a morality clause in your contract, right?"

"It's dinner, not a date." It wasn't like he'd invited her on a yacht. That was only in the dream she had last night.

"It'd better stay that way. He's a volunteer at our facility." She nodded once and then sat back down at her desk. "I retire in a little over a month. If you want to move into this position, you need to prove that you will maintain good ethical standing. People in the community will talk."

That's why she'd mentioned it, to begin with. She didn't want her director to find out from someone else and assume the worst.

"I understand." Mara turned on her heel and left the room, a little deflated. She hadn't had any real expectations of Rian's interest in her, but she at least wanted to enjoy her one dinner. Morality clause. That was code for *you better not sleep with him.*

Dejected, she left the office. She'd have to make it clear to Rian that this was a casual dinner. Nothing else.

The kitchen had erupted into straight chaos. Rian in the middle of it, either participating or trying to stop it. Hard to tell. Several of the boys had found the flour and threw handfuls of it at each other, creating a white cloud.

"Boys!" She took a step in their direction and got a face full.

She closed her eyes. This was not happening.

The room fell silent.

Someone snickered. She snapped her eyes open,

wanting to take her wrath out on whoever thought it was funny.

Rian.

Rian was the one with a hand over his mouth, trying not to laugh but doing a poor job of hiding it.

"Oh. This is funny to you?" She reached out and grabbed her handful of flour and tossed it in his face. He tried to block it, but it's flour, so, really, what the hell could he have blocked?

"You just threw flour at me." His shocked expression made him look a little like a ghost.

With their eyes wide, the kids watched the two adults. Sometimes she wondered if she was the best role model for these kids. Could she handle being the director when she couldn't even control a small room full of children?

She didn't see the flour before it hit the side of her face.

Blair stood there, a gap-toothed grin stretched across her face.

Rian laughed again.

Hell. Mara took a massive handful and threw it. Not at Rian, but at Romeo. He stood off to the side with his typical annoyed, too-cool-for-school expression in place. Until the flour hit him.

Mara leaned toward him, ignoring his angry scowl, and whispered, "Hey—" she winked "—food fight."

The first smile she'd seen in a month appeared on his face. He snatched the flour from another kid and began pelting everyone. All the kids joined in.

Rian seemed to alternate between aiming for her and tossing it softly at Blair.

The boys went to war, hiding behind chairs, ducking between the cabinets.

Rian moved closer, his hand touching her shoulder. "This isn't how I normally cook," he said between laughs.

She waved her hand in front of her face, trying to clear out the flour to see him better. "Really? Because it seemed as though you enjoyed hitting me with it."

A shrill whistle sounded. Both adults and all the children froze in place. Mara winced and slowly turned to see Mrs. Peterson in the doorway, her signature "look" of disapproval in place.

"Mara. Mr. O'Keeley. I'm not sure what's happening here." Her voice was tight and controlled. She wanted to yell, and if Rian hadn't been there, she would have screamed. A lot.

Rian's chest brushed along Mara's spine. He'd moved to stand right behind her. Maybe to support her? He didn't have to. He could have easily walked away.

"I enjoy watching kids have fun in the kitchen," he said, the edge of amusement still in his voice.

The kids snickered. Mara caught herself before she joined in. Mrs. Peterson's expression darkened, reminding her of the Wicked Witch from *Wizard of Oz*.

"I expect you and the kids to clean up, Mara. Six weeks. Remember that."

Wow, she even sounded like that witch.

"I'll help," Rian said.

Mrs. Peterson shook her head. "No. There's no need. I don't think that cooking lessons are the right fit for our program. I appreciate you coming and trying."

She disappeared from the doorway, without the red smoke the *original* witch used. The room remained silent. Disappointment covered each child's face. She hated it.

"C'mon, y'all. Let's clean up." Not surprisingly, Mara's tone lacked enthusiasm.

The kids groaned and started complaining about Rian leaving.

Mara turned around. He stood so close. She tilted her head up, expecting to say something, apologize for Mrs. Peterson's rude dismissal, but her mind blanked.

Completely flat-lined.

He brushed the back of his fingers across her cheek. "You are covered in flour," he murmured.

She wanted to do the same to him, but she interlaced her fingers behind her back and stepped away. She wanted the director's job more.

"I'm sorry this didn't work out," she said. "And I should probably back out on dinner tonight. I have a lot going on in my life."

He watched her for a long second. "I fly out tomorrow morning." He didn't give her a chance to respond. "Lisbon. I have an event."

"Oh—"

"Then I go from there to Melbourne."

"That's a lot of time zones."

He nodded and set his hands on his hips. Covered in flour and he still made her heart race. "Then, I'm back in Atlanta for a couple of weeks."

The kids around them had started picking up overturned chairs, and one of them got the broom. She'd help in a moment after she could move. His eyes were a beautiful shade of green in this light. Earlier, they'd looked blue.

"Then where are you off to?"

"San Francisco."

"For an event?"

His lips twitched, but he didn't smile. "Yes."

"So, you're saying I may never see you again?"

"It's a possibility." He skimmed his fingertips down the outside of her arm.

"I'd still like for you to come to O'Keeley's tonight."

That gorgeous man still wanted to take her out. She let out a shaky breath. It'd be one night with him. She'd read between the lines on that one. She swallowed over her dry throat, hoping she'd make the right decision.

3

"You asked me to come in. Here I am." Rian plopped down in the leather seat, facing his brothers. The office at O'Keeley's Irish Pub had turned into a family gathering place as well as for business. He usually enjoyed seeing his family. After Mara's refusal to go on a date, he wanted to be alone.

Rian crossed his ankle over his knee. "What's the big announcement?"

"What the hell put you in a mood?" Cathal, his younger brother, asked as he sipped a glass of whiskey. With his feet propped up on the coffee table in the office at O'Keeley's, he looked too damn relaxed and happy. And it pissed Rian off.

"None of your damn business."

Cathal smirked. "Touchy."

"We'll get to the announcement in a second." Selena walked to the sofa, curling up in the corner against Brogan's side. "I thought you were supposed to have a date tonight." She looked more amused than concerned. "Did it fall through?"

"Yes," Rian answered, hating to take his bad mood out

on her. "We had an incident at the after-school center today. I asked her out again, and she declined the second time. Said her life was too complicated for the likes of me."

She might not have said those exact words, but that was Mara's meaning. He'd hoped by showing her he wouldn't be around later, that maybe it wouldn't pressure her into thinking he planned some long-term relationship. It'd worked with most of the other women he dated.

One night. No strings attached.

It seemed to scare her off.

"There are other women out there, Rian." Cathal held up his glass. "Come out with me tonight. I have a redhead I need to bother."

Selena pursed her lips together a moment. "The bartender at Fiona's? Why are you bothering her? She helped us after that situation with Simmons."

"It's Fiona, herself. She owns the bar. The pretty woman won't give me the time of day. I stop in there once a week just to try again." Cathal nodded at Rian. "Unlike him, I'm persistent."

"You're just bothersome," Brogan replied, his scowl aimed at his phone instead of at Rian or Cathal for once. "Well, isn't this a piece of shit."

Rian sat forward, as did Cathal. "What?" They replied in unison, before sending each other an annoyed glance. They were eleven months apart and acted more like twins than either one of them would admit. Sometimes Rian wondered what'd possessed his parents to have children so close together, especially when Cathal was the result.

"This food critic, Tiffany McKnight, has written a *horrible* article about us," Brogan said.

Ah. So Brogan finally discovered the nasty review. Rian let his head drop. "I know. I saw it the day I flew back." The food was his responsibility. He'd been slammed for various things in the past by food critics, every chef had, but it didn't mean he enjoyed the feedback.

And Tiffany McKnight seemed particularly lethal in delivering her critiques.

"Read it to us," Selena said. "We all want to hear. I might have to put on my VP of Advertising hat and do damage control."

Brogan shot her a long, sideways glance. "She says that the atmosphere is as boring as the food. Nothing original. Overpriced." He paused and grimaced. "And their chef is too busy promoting himself to give a flying flip about his restaurant."

"A flying flip," Rian muttered.

Selena blinked. "Oh. That's a polite way of saying that you don't give a flying—"

"Selena!" Brogan's shocked expression made Cathal laugh.

Rian wasn't in the mood to laugh. He did care about his restaurant. Their restaurant. Brogan managed it. Cathal drank the whiskey. Rian created the menu.

Boring?

He knew it.

"Don't let it get to you." Selena gave him a sympathetic look he didn't want.

"Well, she's posted this on several websites." Brogan's gaze held Rian's. "And this isn't the first time she's criticized us. She did it last month, too. I just didn't see it."

Rian had seen that one as well.

"You didn't work on your honeymoon?" Cathal slapped his hands on his cheeks. "I'm shocked. You said her name was Tiffany McKnight? Sounds Scottish. Is there a picture of her?"

"Don't even try it." Brogan's stern expression faulted with Selena's light laugh.

Rian couldn't make light of the situation. He had traveled extensively and had no plans to stop. His upcoming schedule included traveling over the next two months. And he's been gone more than at home over the past few years. But staying in one place made him feel claustrophobic. He'd outrun the memories of his past so far, successfully.

"Maybe I do need to stay here more."

Cathal and Brogan shared a glance. He knew what that meant. They both had an opinion on the subject but wouldn't share it. Not entirely. They'd always walked the line with his past, and he appreciated it.

His brothers might irritate him, but they loved each other.

Brogan shifted, taking his arm from around Selena and leaning forward. "I don't like this any more than you do, but there are other options. You don't have to stop your travels. It's one critic. We can add a few things to the menu. Selena already added a live band to Saturday night. That starts tomorrow. We have customers. We stay busy. One critic won't change that."

Selena's focus remained on Rian before glancing at Brogan. "Why are you pushing back from him being here more? I figured you'd want him to stay home and help out. What am I missing?"

"Nothing," all three men said at once.

Rian leaned back. Selena was family now. Maybe it was time she knew.

She stood. "Don't push me out. Please. I love being a part of this family. What happened, Rian? I know Brogan's issue with control. I know that Cathal will turn into the Hulk out of the blue."

"I like that analogy," he said, smiling like an idiot. "That's like being a superhero, right?"

Selena ignored Cathal, her gaze locked onto Rian like a dog with a rabbit. "You. Why do you travel so much? Why is your apartment so sterile? Why don't you ever talk about any women you date?"

"You're too observant," Rian muttered, his mind already traveling down the dark memories.

"I'm just interested. Not only in Brogan but in both of you." Selena crossed her arms. "I've tried squeezing it out of your brother, but he won't budge."

Brogan watched Rian for a long second before saying, "It's not my story to tell."

No. It wasn't. Rian needed to be the one to explain his past to Selena. "You're right, Selena. You are entitled."

Rian leaned back, confiscated Cathal's whiskey, and downed the rest of the amber liquid. He needed something to get him through the retelling of it. His brothers would try to leave it buried. But if he needed to stay in one place, to have some semblance of a steady life to focus on their restaurant, then he needed to face it. If only to let Selena understand and then he'd push it way down deep, again.

"I was married."

Her mouth dropped open as she sat back down. "Oh, my God. When?"

"Shortly after I turned eighteen. I got my girlfriend pregnant; married her the day after she told me."

"You have a child?" She shot an accusatory glare in his direction. "Where is he or she?"

Brogan nudged her, and she stopped her questions.

Cathal poured Rian another drink from the bottle sitting on the table.

"The child was born with a condition," Rian said, taking

the glass from Cathal. The liquid vibrated from the slight tremor in his hand. This was why he traveled. Kept himself busy. Kept everything impersonal. Quick, easy relationships. Superficial friendships.

He couldn't handle the memories. It didn't matter how long it'd been. Last year, ten years, twenty- the pain never went away.

He took a sip. Both Brogan and Cathal kept their gazes averted. The situation affected them almost as deeply.

"My daughter didn't make it past the first couple of hours."

Selena stared at him. Not with pity. Maybe anger for the situation. He wished he could feel the anger. Not the hurt. Pain. Heartbreak.

"I held her. They do that, you know. Let you hold the baby. I know to someone who hasn't been through it, it sounds morbid. Maybe it was. But I'd felt that child grow. Kick." He took a sip, letting the burn trail down his tight throat. "She looked perfect to me. It was a neural tube defect." He'd not tried to understand it then and couldn't think about it now. Knowing what happened, why it happened, didn't change the outcome. He blew out a long breath. "I got a divorce the next month. We weren't really in love. Friends more than anything by that point. I left for culinary school. Cathal had his trouble the next year. Then we moved to America. Left it all behind."

Selena patted Brogan's thigh. Yes. He needed the support as well. He'd shouldered everything to take care of him and Cathal in their worst possible times.

"I'm sorry, Rian. Really." She walked around the coffee table. He rose to meet her, knowing she'd hug him. And, damn it, he wanted it right then.

"Come out with me tonight." Cathal's voice had lost its

usual humor. His cobalt blue eyes looked nearly black in the dim light. "It'll do you good. The noise and the distraction."

"I might do that." Rian finished the second whiskey and handed the glass back. "I might need to get absolutely scuttered before my flight tomorrow. I don't anticipate sleep will come easily." Never did on the days he faced his past.

"I didn't mean to bring all this up by asking you to come here." Selena clasped her hands together and looked back at Brogan.

Her unusual nervousness put Rian on edge. He set a hand on her shoulder, giving her a small squeeze. "What was your announcement, Selena? I've dumped my baggage at your feet and ruined the reason for calling us together?"

She scrunched up her nose like a little bunny rabbit. "It can wait. Really."

"No. Don't change anything because of my baggage. You were bound to hear it eventually. At least I have Cathal for entertainment for the rest of the evening. What was it?"

"In consideration of your baggage, it's actually a pretty crappy time to announce it."

She looked back at Brogan again, her hand resting on her stomach. Her cheeks were flushed, and his gaze dropped down to the cup of tea on the table.

Rian grinned. "You're pregnant?"

"Yes. I'm sorry—"

Rian snatched her back into a hug. "No apologies. The two don't even compare." And they didn't. His history had nothing to do with knowing he'd have a little niece or nephew to spoil. To teach. Selena being pregnant was happy news.

Cathal jumped up. "Man, that was quick. But, you know, Brog is almost an old man."

"I just turned thirty-eight," he grumbled.

Rian passed Selena to Cathal. He embraced her as well. "You should try for back-to-back kids, like Rian and me. Best decision my parents ever made."

"Eleven months apart," Brogan clarified. "And no. I saw what you both put Ma through. I'm not doing that to Selena. Let's start with one."

"It's early, still. But I wanted to tell you." She pursed her lips together the way she always did when she thought about something. "I'm still really sorry about what happened to you, Rian."

"We don't have to bring it up again." Sooner or later he'd have to face his demons and not run from them. That's all he'd done since leaving Ireland. Stay busy. Work hard. Avoid any sort of personal attachments, except for his brothers, and now Selena. Those were the only people he needed in his life.

"So, are we off to the bar?" Cathal pounded on Rian's back. "We can go celebrate the good news instead of drowning out the bad. Better for the digestion, anyhow."

"I suppose I'm in for a night with Cathal." He looked between Brogan and Selena. "You both let us know if you need anything." He stepped across to Brogan and gave him a hard hug. "This is great."

Brogan nodded, averting his eyes. The loss still weighed heavy on everyone's minds, but Brogan would pull it together for Selena. They made a good team.

"If we leave, we might find you a pretty girl to hug on instead of having to settle for your old, married brother." Cathal jingled his keys. "I'll even be your DD."

"I thought Fiona's bar was around the corner from your condo?" Rian walked out of O'Keeley's behind Cathal and into the unexpected chilly night. Finally. He enjoyed living in Atlanta, but he'd always take relief from the oppressive heat and humidity.

"It is. I meant I'd drive us there. After that, it's up to you to get yourself home. Or you can crash at my apartment." He winked. "Or whichever lady you might find."

"I'm sure as hell not sleeping at your apartment. I might not make it out alive. And I'm not out looking for a hookup. I'll leave that to you." There was only one woman who'd satisfy him, and he didn't even have her number for a *third attempt*. Mara intrigued him. He just had a while to wait until he had a chance to try again.

4

———

Her dress was too tight. Her top too low. Her hair looked horrible. Her makeup felt greasy.

"Stop fidgeting. You look cute, Mara." Rachel pulled her long, dark hair over one shoulder and strutted down the sidewalk like it was her personal catwalk.

Once, Mara had tried to imitate her. That hadn't turned out as she'd planned. Instead of the guy across the street noticing her, a police officer asked her to do a field sobriety test.

Mara sighed as she caught her reflection in front of a dark store window. "You think I look cute? Puppies are cute." She'd questioned her sanity at least ten times since leaving the house. Rachel was her best friend in Atlanta. She always dressed amazingly. She could pull off wearing leggings and a cute shirt. Anything on Rachel's model height looked good. Mara, on the other hand, looked more like a stumpy pear when she wore those tunic shirts.

So, she'd worn a dress to prove that she wasn't a stumpy pear. And since it was Georgia, the September weather decided to turn chilly out of nowhere. That made her a stumpy pear in a dress that wanted to be at home wearing sweatpants, microwaving a frozen chicken pot pie for supper.

"Maybe you'll find a guy that likes puppies." Rachel bumped Mara's shoulder. "C'mon. You look great. Have fun tonight. I know I'm not some hot Irish guy that asked you out and for some dumb reason you declined—"

"I'm not dumb. I might have been dumb at the time. But as a general rule, I'm not dumb."

"I don't know why you didn't call him and tell him you changed your mind."

Because she wouldn't ask Mrs. Peterson for his number off his volunteer application. Not after the second lecture she'd received. Apparently, she had a professionalism clause in her contract as well. Unprofessional and immoral. Those two words had never applied to Mara before.

Mrs. Peterson had reminded her for a fourth time about the director's position. Applying for the job just turned into a six-week audition. Giving into Rian might feel good, damn good, but at the same time, her future would slip away. No man was worth that.

"Where are we going? I'm tired of walking."

"You sound like a whiny kid." Rachel patted Mara on the back. "Just a little bit farther, sweetheart."

Mara pouted and crossed her arms. Uncomfortable, hungry, and without a sexy Irishman. That would make any woman cranky. She could at least solve two of the three if she were at home.

"Here. Let's have a drink." Rachel opened the door to a bar and motioned Mara in first. "It will put you in a better mood."

"It looks like a dump," she mumbled, hopefully low enough the bouncer checking IDs at the door didn't hear.

He was big, bald, and had so many tattoos covering his arms that Mara couldn't begin to describe one of them.

He barely glanced at her ID. That was because of Rachel. She turned heads everywhere she went.

"One drink, Rach. Then we're out. You promised me a jazz club and low key. Not—this." The music reminded her of high school, and the disco ball didn't help the atmosphere. The bar was eclectic. That was the best term she could use. Random memorabilia hung from the ceiling. A lamp. Some Mardi Gras beads. Complete with a tricycle mounted in the corner.

It smelled like beer and—something sweet? Odd combination.

"There they are."

Mara didn't bother looking for whoever "they" were. She glared at Rachel and kept herself from stomping her foot in annoyance. "You set us up with guys?"

"Yup. That's the best way for you to get over your guy."

"He's not my guy."

Rachel lifted a shoulder. "You are obviously miserable you didn't go out with him. The guy I met on that dating app had a friend he wanted to bring along. Ooh, his friend is cute, too. How does he compare to the Irish chef?"

Mara followed her gaze. The guys were decent. Rachel's man was of medium height with a tan complexion.

The man there for Mara fell pretty short of her low standards in the looks department. But, seriously, Denzel Washington could have asked her for her number, and she'd still felt like crap after watching Rian walk out of her life.

Rachel just didn't understand.

"Here." Mara typed Rian's name into her phone and pulled up a picture of him. "There. That's him."

Her friend's eyes widened. "Hell, Mara, I'd have given up my job to have a night with him."

She looked at his picture on her cell phone. "I started to," she muttered. She'd have hated herself in the morning. One night could have ended her career ambitions. Or at least derailed them until she found another position. She wasn't that adventurous.

Rowdy laughter at the bar caught her attention. She could only see the back of the two men, but the redhead behind the bar didn't look amused. In fact, she seemed utterly annoyed as she threw her hands up and stormed away, leaving them to laugh louder.

Girl, I feel your pain. Because Mara was about to be annoyed by Josh, the accountant with soft hands and soft brown eyes. A soft smile. A soft middle. A soft laugh.

They sat on a low sofa together, the type where it seemed impossible to keep a respectable distance from Josh because of the lack of springs in the cushions. Either that or Josh liked sitting hip-to-hip with her. It didn't matter; she had to smell his cheap cologne that almost reminded her of the perfume her grandmother wore—poor guy.

But Mara tried to play nice for Rachel's sake. She listened to Josh's lame jokes. Nodded at his never-ending stories. And after an hour, her initial assessment of the man held true. Boring. Dull. Nothing like the colorful personality of Rian O'Keeley.

God, Rian would take out a restraining order if he knew how obsessed she'd become in less than a week.

She'd eventually get over the chef, but, for the time being, she'd take wallowing in her sadness. She needed a pity party and chicken pot pie to heal. Not loud music, cheap drinks, and Josh.

"I'm going to go buy the next round," Rachel said,

standing up and hauling Mara to her feet. "Does everyone want the same?"

Josh smiled up at Mara. "I'll have whatever you get, gorgeous."

"Are you sure?"

"That you're gorgeous? Absolutely." He reached out and snagged her hand, kissing the back of it. She managed not to wipe it off on her dress, but the grimace probably slipped through.

"I meant to drink, Josh. I'm not sure what I'm going to get. You could end up with a plain Coke. Possibly water."

"I'm down with whatever you want." He winked like it was some sort of inside, sexual joke. Maybe she'd missed something during one of the last dozen times she'd zoned out. With her luck, she'd consented to something with one of her absent-minded head nods.

She followed Rachel to the bar. "I really like Ben." Rachel waved at the bartender to get her attention. "I think he likes me, too."

"Of course, he does."

Rachel bumped her shoulder. "You looked like you were having a little fun."

Mara blinked, trying to recall ever having that feeling. "Wow. I'm a better actress than I gave myself credit for."

"What do you think of him?"

"Who?"

"Josh," Rachel said, thoroughly exasperated. "He said you were gorgeous. I thought the little hand kiss thing was sweet."

Two hands landed on either side of Mara, boxing her in.

She jumped and froze.

"Yes, Josh does seem sweet."

Rian.

Of all the hole-in-the-wall bars in Atlanta...

She turned within his arms and forced her gaze up. In the low light of the spinning disco ball, he looked like a fallen angel. His light brown hair was mussed a little. The angles of his face made him look a bit dangerous. Calling him sexy was an underrated adjective.

"Breathe, honey," Rachel cooed beside her.

She took a deep, lung filling breath. Mistake. It filled her head with his scent. Something that smelled a little like the ocean on a warm day. How did he find a cologne that matched his eyes?

He trailed a finger down her cheek. "I see you got all the flour off."

Mara swallowed and nodded. He made her mind stop functioning. Really. Just a big, blank, empty void.

"If you didn't want to see me, because of Josh, you could have said so. I can take rejection."

She shook her head, finally finding her voice. "I wasn't told about Josh until an hour ago."

He smiled a little lopsided grin. He was drunk. Or at least a level past tipsy.

Mara licked her lips.

His eyes zeroed in on the movement. Why was this man so interested in her? No. She shouldn't question it. Go with the flow. Rachel always complained she wasn't spontaneous.

"Mara, what are you ordering? Josh said he'd drink what you did." Rachel tapped Rian on the shoulder. "Remember, Josh is her date. Not you."

"That's unfortunate," he replied. "But since I'm here and Josh is still sitting on his arse, I'll buy your drink. What will you have, Mara?"

Him. She wanted him.

His eyes narrowed as though he could read her thoughts.

"What are you drinking?" Somehow, it managed to come out sounding decently seductive.

"Because I'm with Cathal, it's whiskey tonight." He shifted a little closer.

She tried to ignore the heat from his body. "That's pretty stereotypical, isn't it? That an Irish guy drinks whiskey?"

"My brother proudly lives up to almost every stereotype possible." He set his hand on her waist. "Would you like one?"

"One what?"

He grinned. "A glass of whiskey?"

"Yes." And she hoped like hell it tasted better than cheap whiskey she'd drank in college. She'd never recover from the embarrassment if she gagged in front of him.

He glanced up at the bartender. "Darling, give her the same as Cathal and me."

"On your tab?" the bartender asked.

"Yes."

"What about Josh?" There was no mistaking the humor in the bartender's voice. "Poor guy might need a bottle of whiskey after watching you seduce his date. He doesn't know whether to storm over here and break this up or leave. He's stood up three times already and then sat back down."

"He wanted what she had," Rachel chimed in.

"Charge that to his tab," Rian added.

The bartender leaned on the bar. "Shouldn't we ask him first?"

"No."

"Your call. If he refuses to pay, I'm sticking it on Cathal's tab. He can pay for your expensive joke."

"That's fine." Rian shifted, close enough for his warm

body to lightly graze hers. A shiver she failed to contain raced down her spine. "Come stay with me tonight, Mara."

Her brain tried to catch up to his offer. Her body had its own answer. Warmth traveled through her limbs, making them feel loose like she'd already had the glass of whiskey.

Rachel and the bartender both paused and seemed to wait for her answer as well. She didn't want to be in a relationship again, not like the one she'd had with Shane, so this should be perfect. One night filled with Rian.

But she wasn't made for that. That's why she'd refused him the second time he'd offered her a date.

"If I can't have that—" he leaned down "—then send me on my way."

Her breath stalled as she waited. Her hands gripped the bar behind her like a lifeline. When a man as gorgeous as Rian kisses, he blurs the line between a dream world and reality.

Her eyes drifted closed, and for the moment, she let go.

His lips were soft. The whiskey on his tongue sweet.

His hands cupped her cheeks. His thumbs brushed along the side of her temples. Over and over, he kissed her.

And the man didn't just kiss. He made it a damned art form.

And she could do nothing but kiss him back and hold on for dear life.

When his hard body pressed completely against hers, the terrible music blasting over the speakers covered the moan that slipped out.

He pulled back. His eyes, the color of moss in the dark light, held hers. The kiss seemed to sober him.

Her head continued to spin.

"Have a good night, Mara." He took one step back before he turned and strode out of the bar.

The three women watched the door where he'd exited.

"Holy shit," Rachel muttered.

"I agree," the bartender added. She rolled her eyes. "Too bad his brother isn't that seductive. More like a pain in the ass."

Rachel spun around. "Brother? He has a brother."

"He left, too." She held out her hand. "I'm Fiona, by the way. I own the bar."

"Mara."

"I gathered that."

Mara looked at the two whiskeys sitting on the bar. "Did he just stiff you?"

"No." Fiona waved her hand toward the cash register. "They have a credit card permanently on file. I usually charge the brother an outrageous tip for making me listen to his bullshit once a week. I'm either treated to it Friday or Saturday night, but like a recurring infection, he makes an appearance."

"I'll have to remember that," Rachel mumbled before she straightened her shoulders. "Time to get back to Josh." Rachel tried for a smile, but it came out like a grimace. "That's a pretty sad way to follow up an amazing goodbye kiss."

Goodbye kiss. It had been. Rian left in the morning. This was Atlanta. No way they'd run into each other again.

5

Three weeks of traveling left Rian tired and irritable. Living in hotel rooms never bothered him. Not seeing his family, eating on the road, he handled. But he'd returned home with the same damn problem.

He'd played with recipes. Dozens of them. Nothing spectacular to introduce into the restaurant, only average tastes that didn't set O'Keeley's apart.

With the nights cooling off, finally, he had more options with the menu—different flavors and ingredients. Nothing like the new fusion he searched for, but *something* unique on the menu might bring it back to life.

The kitchen at O'Keeley's was empty early Saturday morning. Selena and Brogan would arrive in a couple of hours. The kitchen staff to prep after that. He'd work until he figured out a new special to offer next week and give them time to order the ingredients.

The damn food critic's words tore a hole in his confidence. Not that he'd share that with anyone.

Boring.

No one else could fix that except Rian.

Rian worked for the next two and a half hours. By a half-past eight, six options sat underneath the warmer. He wanted Brogan to try them, even if they weren't precisely breakfast food.

"Rian?" Selena's voice called for him as she pushed through the door. "It smells amazing in here. What have you cooked?"

He walked her through the different dishes. The first was a lamb dish he always made for Cathal when he felt charitable. It wasn't fancy or anything special. Leeks. Turnips. Tasty flavors that stood on their own. At least in his opinion. He'd mainly cooked that one because he'd wanted to eat it and had saved a portion in the fridge for his lunch later.

Selena went right for it.

"Breakfast of champions," she mumbled.

Brogan came in without a word and picked up a different dish.

"I love this!" Selena pointed at the lamb.

Rian chuckled. "I was worried neither one of you would try my dishes seeing as it's not even nine in the morning."

Selena kept her head bent over the plate, her entire focus on the lamb. "We got, um, a little caught up this morning. Didn't manage to have breakfast."

Brogan made a face.

Rian pointed at the plate Brogan held in his hand. "I almost stopped you when you picked it up."

"And that just confirmed I hate beets, no matter the time of day. I didn't see the beets. No beets. I'm not serving anything I can't pronounce or stomach." Brogan picked a piece of lamb off Selena's plate. "This, on the other hand, is a go for me. You know you have Cathal's vote."

They tried the other ones but kept coming back to the

same dish. Selena shifted, blocking her plate from Brogan and finishing the lamb herself.

Rian walked to the fridge and pulled out his plate for lunch. He hated microwaving food in general, but since his brothers didn't mind, he put it in for thirty seconds before passing it to Brogan.

"Here's another serving."

Brogan took it and then blocked Selena when she tried to take a bite off his plate.

"It seems the lamb wins. We'll give it a try. I'll invite the food critic back." Rian leaned on the counter. "I wish we could put someone undercover near her. We don't know who served her last time, so we can't use one of the staff members. I want to know if she eats all her food. If she's taking notes. If she looks to be a generally unpleasant human."

Selena finally managed to score a bite of Brogan's lamb. She chewed and nodded. "I saw her picture. I'll be her waitress. I know I didn't serve her before." Selena took Brogan's nearly empty plate and scraped the last of the lamb from it, looking far too tempted to lick the remnants.

Both men watched her.

She grinned. "What? The baby obviously likes their uncle's cooking. Oh, Rian. I almost forgot. A few of the kids and their families came in with those gift certificates you provided to them. I hated it when a couple of them asked for you, and you weren't here. But I gave them free dessert, so I'm fairly certain, to them at least, they were happier than getting to see you again."

"Ha. Ha." He began stacking the plates to wash them. "Did you see the director that came in with them before?" He'd thought about Mara daily, and he wasn't sure he liked the effect she'd had on him. It threw his well-organized mind out of sync.

She made a little humming sound. "She might have come in here. And she might have asked if you were back in town. Her waitress told me."

"Who are you talking about?" Brogan wiped his mouth with a napkin. "Or do I care about this at all?"

"No, you don't," Rian responded. "How long ago was that?"

"Two days."

He'd just missed her.

"I went out to meet her and told her when you'd fly in. I wasn't sure when you were working but that you'd be around town at least."

"Did she seem happy about that?"

Brogan's eyebrows pulled down low. "Geez, man. You sound like a primary school kid. Are you going to ask if she'll meet you under the slide, too?"

"I will if she'll meet me there." Rian didn't care about what his older brother thought about Mara at the moment. Or more it seemed his infatuation with Mara.

"I think she's very pretty," Selena said.

"Me, too." Although pretty was somewhat of an understatement. He'd had several opportunities to take women out while he was traveling, but because of that kiss with Mara, he wasn't interested.

He wanted to relive that kiss.

And more.

He wanted more and knew she wasn't the type of woman who'd skip right along into his bed. He hardly dated in Atlanta and never brought them back to his place. Not that his condo was anything sacred. Everyone teased him about his lack of decorating. That's fine. He didn't need personal effects. Not when his family was right there.

And if he ever got nostalgic, he went to Brogan's condo. The similarities to their parents' house back in Ireland took away the feelings of homesickness.

And he did go back to Ireland. He'd not mentioned it much, but when he traveled that way, he stayed in their old house. Brogan brought half the furniture to America, none of them knew what they'd do with the land when they first left, but since they kept it, Rian had the house refurbished.

Selena clapped her hands together. "I've got it. Why don't you ask Mara to come back on Saturday? That way, you can see her, *and* she can help eavesdrop on our food critic."

Brogan wrapped an arm around Selena's waist. "That would be a good plan, actually. The whole two birds, one stone. You get to see her again, and she can help us out."

Rian's lips twitched, trying to contain his amusement with Brogan. "You care about helping me out with a woman?"

"A woman like that Camille that busted in during the party a couple of months ago...no. Not at all. Someone that seems as nice as Mara, based on what Selena said, yes. You deserve someone sweet, too."

"I'm not looking for long-term." He crossed his arms. "I don't want to settle down in one place." They all knew he just didn't want to slow down long enough to possibly relive the past. Either in his head or reality, if that situation struck again, he couldn't survive a second time.

"But I would like to see Mara again."

Selena wiggled her eyebrows. "Cathal told me about the kiss you gave her at the bar. I imagine she'll be willing to help us out for a second chance."

"Cathal needs to stop gossiping."

Brogan sighed. "You know that will never happen."

"No," Rian said. He set his hands on the counter. "I don't suppose it will. Alright, I'll stop by the after-school program tomorrow. Take something easy to make for the kids." He covered up a laugh. That didn't involve flour. And for the first time in a while, he had a rush of nerves. What if she turned him down...again?

He pushed that from his mind. Women turned him down in the past. It'd never bothered him before. He didn't fly through women the way Cathal did. That required too much energy.

But why wouldn't Mara go to dinner with him? She'd kissed him back. He hadn't imagined it. Cathal had asked, several times, why Rian had given up. For Cathal, the chase entertained him as much as the women. That's why he bothered the owner at Fiona's every week.

Mara didn't play those games.

She might look shy and sweet, but he knew she wasn't a pushover.

Selena set both hands on the stainless-steel counter, mimicking his stance. "Will you take some advice?"

"From my wise sister? Of course."

Brogan harrumphed and crossed his arms. "I tried to offer you advice yesterday, and you told me you didn't need anyone's opinion."

"That was selective hearing on your part, Brog. I said I didn't want *your* opinion. Selena is different."

She waved her hand at Brogan. "I'm a female. I think I'm better suited to giving him advice on Mara."

"I managed to make you fall in love with me." Brogan leaned down to kiss his wife.

She turned her cheek. "And managed almost to lose me

in the process. Now, Rian, when you ask her about helping us with the food critic, make sure she knows that you want *her* there. You don't want her to feel like you're asking her as a friend. But don't put too much pressure on her. She needs to know you want her without scaring her into a corner."

"I think I know how to talk to a woman and make my intentions clear, Selena."

Selena arched an eyebrow, her lips pressing together.

Damn, but the woman was already ready to be a mother. "Fine. I'll try to remember that." He looked over Selena's head to Brogan. "I still don't know how you managed to find a woman bossier than yourself."

Brogan grinned and dropped an arm across Selena's shoulders. "She's perfect."

Rian had to agree that Selena was perfect for his brother. Rian took the dishes to the sink. He usually washed his plates, but at the moment, he only had Mara on his mind.

He walked out of the kitchen and, surprisingly, Cathal walked into the restaurant. A cup of coffee in one hand and his briefcase in his other.

And sunglasses still in place.

"You look like the poster child for a hungover businessman."

Cathal set his briefcase down on the closest table and shot him a bird.

"Classy."

"I'd yell, but that wouldn't help the headache." He sat down at the bar, dropping his head onto the wood.

Rian leaned beside him. "Why do you do it to yourself?"

"Do what?" Cathal asked, his voice muffled against his arm.

"Drink that much. How many times have you gone out this week?"

"Four."

Rian sat down in the chair beside him, looking out over the empty dining room. He folded his hands in his lap. He was rarely serious with his younger brother, although he understood part of what Cathal had gone through having his own memories to run from.

"Do you think you should talk to someone about it?"

The "it" in question was his past.

"Don't you?" was the muffled reply.

"I'm not killing my liver every night of the week."

"You also don't know your days of the week as four is not seven, and therefore it is not every day of the week." He sat up and sipped his coffee. "And this isn't all from drinking. I couldn't sleep again last night."

"I didn't know you had a problem with sleeping. We always assumed you came in looking like shit because you were hungover." Rian itched to get Brogan, drag him into the conversation. First, Cathal never opened up. Second, Brogan handled everything when it came to them both. Most of the time, it bothered him, but having to be the mature one and make sure Cathal was okay made Rian uncomfortable. He could screw up and make it worse.

Cathal took his sunglasses off. God, yes, the man looked exhausted. "It's easier to play it off that way than to face it head-on." He cut his eyes Rian's direction. "You know?"

Rian nodded. He knew. That's why he exhausted himself with work. That was his release. Cathal didn't seem to have the same focus.

"Do you have to go to work today?"

Cathal drank the last of his coffee and set the cup down the same way he might an empty pint at a bar. "Yes. They seem to think I do well with divorce cases. I hate the shit. Over two-thirds of the time, husbands are to blame; it's a wonder how the women lasted as long as they had. It's an act of control to keep my mouth closed and my tongue still."

"You can't save the world, Cathal."

"No. But I can't turn away when I see it happening." He picked at the paper surrounding the coffee cup. "I sometimes wonder what Ma would say."

"Not Da?"

Cathal cut his eyes at Rian. "No. He wasn't the caring type, was he? But Ma would either take one of two roads. Be sympathetic with us. Make us something good to eat. Invite us back into the house until she thought us well enough to leave."

"Or," Rian said, standing up off the barstool. "She'd tell that a new day has started, and we better get our sorry butts out the door before it passes us by. I can't tell you it will get better, but you can call me if you need to. Or come over. You know that."

"I do, but it's nice to hear all the same."

Rian patted him on the back and left him at the bar. It seems as though he and Brogan had a few more things to learn about Cathal.

6

The kids hated her. At least, for the moment, it felt that way. Mara clapped her hands. "Quiet!" Her shout landed on deaf ears. Or maybe they really didn't hear her. Because they'd started another round of dodge ball in the big, open gymnasium area and even with two kids now crying, and one in the bathroom hiding, the boys weren't slowing down.

She let her head fall back and stared at the ceiling. She made a difference in children's lives. If she were in charge of the center, those dodge balls would mysteriously all end up in the dumpster.

The sudden silence sounded as loud as a shout.

She looked around, not knowing what to expect. Maybe blood on the floor from another ball to the face. Perhaps a ball to *her* face. Wouldn't surprise her at this point in the day.

She blinked at the man standing at the entrance.

Rian O'Keeley, looking like a model, stood with a grocery bag in each hand. The grocery store down the street should consider him for their marketing campaign. She might venture out of the frozen food aisle with his image plastered around the store.

He smiled at the kids who'd gathered around him and began firing their questions, one after another. He laughed, deep and rich as if he didn't have a care in the world.

His skin looked a little tan. Golden. Probably from wherever he'd traveled. But why was he here? Now? She'd finally made it to O'Keeley's and subtly asked about his whereabouts. Had they told him?

Rian moved into the gym, his gaze locked on her although he responded to the kids' questions.

She licked her lips, considering how to greet him. A kiss wasn't appropriate. Not here and not anytime. It'd been a mistake before.

No. Not a mistake. Wrong description. More like regret. Because after that kiss, she'd not been able to think of a man, look at a man, damn, not even dream of a man without Rian's eyes and that kiss popping into her mind. For nearly three weeks.

It was like he'd given her a medical condition.

"Mara. Hi." He held up the two bags. "I wanted to try to teach the kids again if you don't mind. I would have called, but I didn't have your number." He grinned, a sexy, half-smile that made her toes curl. "Which I'd like to have if you don't mind."

That was the smoothest way to ask for a woman's number she'd ever heard.

"Nice to see you," she began, her voice a little higher than usual. "I'm sure they'll all enjoy whatever you brought to eat." She leaned to the side and saw the kids trailing behind him, dodge ball forgotten. "At least you got their attention. I've been trying for the past twenty minutes. The older boys get a little rough playing dodge ball." She pointed to the two kids sniffling in the corner.

"Dodge ball?" He turned to face the kids. "You help make this snack, and while it bakes, I'll beat all of you."

The boys, roughly ages twelve to fourteen, started chattering away with excitement.

He held up his hand. "No. First, we bake."

"Baking is for girls," Romeo said as he bounced the dodge ball. "I bet you don't even know how to play, being a fancy chef, and everything."

"What do you want to bet?"

The guys looked at each other. They didn't have money. Surely Rian knew that.

He leaned down. "I'll tell you what. If you win, then I'll bring you all a pizza after school tomorrow."

"And if we lose?" Romeo asked.

"Then you have to clean the kitchen." He winked. "And I'll still bring you pizza."

Romeo fist-bumped Rian. "Let's go bake so we can kick your butt."

How had he breezed back into the center like he'd never left? She watched him as he walked toward the kitchen. Tall. Strong. Completely drool-worthy. That man had offered her one night.

What the hell was her problem?

He paused by the kitchen door. "Are you coming, Mara?"

She nodded and made her feet move his direction. He stepped back from the door and held out his arm, blocking Romeo from entering.

"Ladies first."

Romeo scrunched his face. "But that's Ms. Mara."

"She's still a lady."

He shrugged. "If you say so."

"Oh—" he paused until she passed by "—I do."

As she caught the ocean scent of his cologne, a sigh slipped from her lips. A weak, fainting sound that was better suited for an eighteenth-century parlor than a modern woman.

The kids stared at Rian, licking their lips in anticipation of food. Her kids were always hungry.

"What are we cooking?" She started unloading the ingredients beside him. His arm brushed against her shoulder. Did he do things like that on purpose? Did he know how it made her feel?

The overwhelming need to press closer against his body was overshadowed by the realization that she didn't compare to the models he dated. But that was his fault for kissing her that way. His fault for making her think she had a real chance.

"Mara?" He angled her direction, his chest brushing her shoulder. "Are you listening?"

He was laughing at her. She could see it in his green eyes. Because today they looked green. "No. I wasn't." She moved to the other side of the counter. Distance was good. "What are we cooking?"

Rian looked at the kids. "Potato bites."

"Like French fries?" Romeo asked. "Because we all love fries."

"No. These are more like potato skins." He pulled out two large bags of red potatoes. "Who will scrub the potatoes?"

When no one volunteered, Mara raised her hand. "I will."

"Good. I'd planned to offer the team captain position to anyone who helped first." He winked.

Romeo stomped his foot. "Hey! I'm always a captain."

"I guess you better volunteer to help out because Ms. Mara is the captain for Team One."

"I don't—"

Rian subtly shook his head at her objection. She'd play along with the cooking game, but there was no way in hell he'd get her out on that court. She wasn't in the mood for Romeo to peg her with a ball. She liked her nose unbroken.

They scrubbed the potatoes and sliced them. Rian demonstrated how to smash and mince the garlic and grate the cheese. They looked like an appetizer she'd find in his restaurant.

Mara glanced around the room. "Hey, has anyone seen Blair?" It didn't take more than three seconds for her stomach to drop. "I'm going to look for her. I thought she came in here with us." And she'd been so focused on Rian.

"No, she didn't." Rian lifted his gaze to meet hers. "I waved to her from the doorway. I think she was sitting at that little table coloring, but she didn't follow you in here."

Mara wiped her hands on the dishtowel and bolted out the door. Blair was nine. She knew not to wander out the front door.

"Blair?" Mara called, standing in the middle of the gymnasium floor, scanning the area. Where would she have gone? Rian's hand landed on her shoulder. She hadn't realized he'd followed her out.

"Why don't you check the toilets? I'll poke my head into those rooms along there." He squeezed her shoulder. "We'll find her."

She moved off toward the bathroom. "Blair?"

The sounds of Blair getting sick hit her before she spotted the little girl's feet facing the toilet underneath the stall door.

"Blair, sweetie, can I get you anything?" She'd always

wanted kids, but at that moment, she was happy only to have her angry-at-the-world cat. Hairballs were better to deal with than this. "I'll be back with some water."

She took a step out of the door and bumped into Rian in the narrow hallway that held the women's restroom. "She's in there. Throwing up."

"Ah, poor thing." He set his hands-on Mara's shoulders. "Do you need help with anything for her?"

She couldn't stand it any longer. He had some agenda. Something propelled him to string her along this way. She moved a step beyond his reach. "Why are you doing this?"

"Helping you because a little girl is sick?"

She crossed her arms and gave him a bland look. "You're far from dumb. You know what I mean. Here. Around me. Touching me."

"Do I really have to explain why I like touching you?"

"Yes! You do. Because it doesn't make a lick of sense." Because look at him. Her fake self-esteem told her that, in theory, she was worthy of anyone, even someone that looked like a model and smelled terrific. Yes. That cologne he wore was lethal. But having someone like him in front of her, holding her, watching her with those blue-green eyes—the reality was harder to swallow than the theory.

"I like you."

"But, you'll end up leaving again soon, right?" Because that's what Rian did. He traveled. All over the world while she was stuck in Georgia, watching other people's children while they threw up in the bathroom a few feet away.

A glamorous life versus hum-drum ordinary.

"Eventually, I will leave, but the restaurant needs me at the moment. I will admit I had a reason to come here today, but I *wanted* to see you, so it was nothing more than an excuse. I'm here to ask for a favor."

At least her suspicions had been correct. He had an agenda. She kept her arms crossed, needing the barrier. "What?"

He laid a hand on her shoulder again. "O'Keeley's has a food critic who's posting some pretty bad things about my food."

Mara nodded. "I saw one yesterday. Tiffany something?"

His gaze darkened. "Yes. That's the—woman," he finally seemed to settle on.

Mara raised her eyebrow. "Were you going to call her something else? I don't agree with her assessment, but just because a female's opinion differs from your own doesn't mean she should be labeled with an ugly word."

He brushed his finger along the curve of her cheek.

Like an idiot, she just stood there because it felt amazing to have him looking at her like that.

"Ah, Mara, you're so fierce. Believe me. My ma would have disowned me for thinking less of females." His voice remained soft and soothing. "And the term I would use if Tiffany were a male name I wouldn't dare utter in your presence. The critique cuts me deep. I've controlled my reaction the best way possible."

Before she stopped herself, she reached out and touched his arm. It was a natural reaction when kids were upset, to pat them on the shoulder. Encourage them. But his shoulder was too high to make a motherly pat possible.

Her subconscious had settled on stroking his bicep, which was also completely inappropriate. "You shouldn't take it personally. I ate at O'Keeley's. Your food is amazing."

The muscle underneath her fingers tightened. "Thank you," he murmured, shifting his body slightly, putting the hallway wall behind her. With another slow step, her back pressed against the cold concrete. "I haven't gotten that kiss out of my head, Mara."

Both her hands gripped his shoulders as a way to steady herself and not sink to the floor. Not that she'd fall if she did let go with his body tight against hers.

"What was the favor?" If she kept talking, then maybe she wouldn't close her eyes and put her job and future on the line by kissing him with Mrs. Peterson sitting in her office around the corner.

"I did." He leaned down, eyes focused on her lips. "That has nothing to do with this—"

"Ms. Mara?" Blair stood in the doorway to the women's restroom.

Mara jumped.

Rian immediately dropped his hands from her hips and stepped back. She hadn't realized he held her there until his fingers disappeared from her body.

"Blair, darling," Rian said, dropping to her level. "How are you feeling, beautiful?"

"Rotten." She crossed her arms, pouting. "You looked like you were going to kiss Ms. Mara."

Rian's head tilted. "Would that bother you?"

Was he really asking a nine-year-old her opinion on the subject? The man hadn't even asked her thoughts.

"Yes." Blair crossed her arms. "I wanted you to be *my* boyfriend."

His face registered shock before he schooled his features into a playful look. "Of course I'm your boyfriend. In fact, I came to find you because I need to play a game of dodge ball, and since you're sick, I want you to cheer me on." He rose and held out his hand. "Here. We'll find you a spot on the side of the gym where you'll be safely tucked away and might not pass along whatever has you feeling ill." He led Blair out of the hallway.

Hot, sexy Irishman, who kisses like it should be illegal, cooks delicious meals, and is fantastic with kids. Too bad, the perfect man came with a no strings attached warning label.

7

Rian moved in close to Mara. She'd finally come to O'Keeley's. Not to have dinner with him, but to eavesdrop on the food critic. Either way, seeing her again eased the stress of the situation. Some of the tension that'd built up all day drained out of his shoulders when he touched her.

Rian rested his hand along her lower back, pleased she didn't jerk away from him. Her focus remained straight ahead, determined to resist him. Her skin warmed his hand through her thin, red shirt, and it was hard to keep a respectable distance. A date, just the two of them, needed to happen soon. Along with another kiss without the risk of interruption.

The crowd in the restaurant was fairly standard for the middle of the week. Various tables were occupied with either couples or young families. But they'd set Mara and her friend Rachel in a spot near the side and away from the crowds.

"Here's where you'll sit." Rian pulled out the chair for Mara. He leaned close to her neck, enjoying the sweet scent of peaches. "God, you smell delicious, Mara." She cut her eyes over her shoulder, their mouths coming in line. "Have a drink with me after dinner."

"That would be rude to Rachel," Mara said.

Rachel sat down across from her. "No, it wouldn't." She grinned at Rian. "Actually, it would." She winked. "I heard you have a brother."

"I have two, to be exact." Rian stepped to the side, away from the sweet temptation of Mara. "One's married with a babe on the way, and the other isn't anyone you'd be interested in."

"I think you should let me decide that."

Rian didn't need Cathal messing things up with Mara by chasing after her friend.

"Is that the table where Tiffany will be seated? What time should she be here?" Mara avoided his gaze, and he hated it. He wanted to see her face one more time before he had to disappear into the kitchen and await his fate with the food critic.

He paused long enough that she tilted her head up, looking for his answer. "In another thirty minutes. So, no rush on dinner. And everything you order is on the house."

"I like being a part of a covert operation." Rachel wiggled in her seat. "Free food and drinks."

"We appreciate the help. And if you can't tell us anything, that's fine. It's a long shot, I know, but we'd like the upper hand if possible." He leaned down and dropped his voice to a whisper in Mara's ear. "The offer still stands for later." He was one second shy of begging, so he kissed a spot behind her ear that she'd exposed by wearing her hair back. "You do smell amazing."

He left, not waiting on an answer and risking making a scene if he kissed her again. At the door to the kitchen, he glanced over his shoulder. Mara's shell-shocked expression amused him.

Why did his interest in her come as a surprise?

He pushed his way into the kitchen, grabbing an apron and slipping on a baseball hat. Later, he would think about his primal need to see her and her reluctance. Supervising the preparation of the new lamb dish they'd added as tonight's special took priority. His reputation in Atlanta rested on a damn comfort food dish he'd never had any intention to put on the menu.

But Tiffany MacKnight was due any second. She'd refused at first when Selena called her. The critic had claimed she didn't need another opportunity to taste their food, seeing as that was the third time she'd reviewed it. Then Cathal called her. Rian didn't have a clue what the man said to her, but sure enough, he'd managed to get her to agree to come in and give it a try.

Rian was half surprised that Cathal didn't manage to convince Tiffany to go out on a date. Rian snorted and continued prepping the lamb. Maybe he had.

Cathal pushed open the door to the kitchen thirty minutes later. "She's here."

"Great." He kept his head down, working on the line with the other cooks. It was quieter in there when he worked like everyone was afraid to joke and cut up with his presence. Most nights, he'd appreciate them taking their job seriously.

Tonight he wished for the distraction.

Cathal leaned against the wall, a beer in his hand. "By the way, what do you know of the tall brunette sitting across from your Mara?"

"She's not my Mara."

Cathal blinked. "I think you need to claim her or else that makes her fair game, brother."

It was an empty threat. They hadn't fought over a girl since they were fourteen. Mara wasn't Cathal's type, anyway. But Cathal did what Cathal did best: pester the hell out of him and stir up trouble.

"Her friend's name is Rachel."

"Do you mind—"

"Yes, I mind. She's Mara's friend."

"I don't know what you're afraid will happen. Women love me."

Rian smirked. "Except for Fiona."

Cathal took a long drink of his beer. "Yes. Except for her. And I can't stand it. That's why I need Rachel. I need something to boost my confidence. Months and months of being rejected by my redheaded bartender has put a dent in my ego."

Rian continued to work on the line with the other cooks but managed a glance at his brother. "You haven't had a problem with your confidence since you were born. That may be the problem with Fiona. She doesn't want to be lumped in with all the other women you can charm."

"Alright. Then I suppose that means I need to go introduce myself to Rachel. Try my charms out on a different woman."

"No." Rian straightened and stared at Cathal for a long time. "If you screw around with her it might mess things up with Mara. I had a hard enough time getting her to come out after asking her three times." He motioned toward the dining room. "And I'm not even sitting with her, so I hardly call it a proper date."

Cathal groaned and rolled his eyes. "God, you owe me. Those legs—"

He didn't give a shit about Cathal's already full sex life. Rian turned, grabbed a clean plate, and unceremoniously plated a large helping of lamb in the center of the plate. It was meant for a different table, but he could make another one in a few minutes. "Here's my payback."

Cathal's eyes lit up. "Don't tell the women I date that they'll always come second to a good meal. It'd ruin my reputation." He took the plate and left.

The door barely stopped swinging before Selena arrived. "Alright. She ordered the lamb. Did Cathal leave any? I saw that plate he had."

"Yes." Rian blew out a steady breath. "How is Mara's table?"

"Fine. They both cleaned their plates, and I don't think that was an act. The critic has taken two phone calls, so I'm hoping they caught some of her conversations. I lowered down the speaker volume of the music in that corner."

"You are so devious." He pointed at her perfectly flat stomach. "I hope you pass that characteristic on to my niece or nephew. They need some fun in their life, coming from Brogan's gene pool."

"Your brother is fun." She winked. "Just not in a way you get to see."

"Gross." But he grinned. "I'll have her lamb out in fifteen minutes. Watch out for Cathal. He had his eye on Mara's friend, Rachel. If he screws this up, I may disown him."

"Got it. Babysit Cathal, grow a tiny human, wait on your food critic, handle Brogan's mood—" she smiled, incredibly fake "— and look happy doing it all." She hip-checked the door and called over her shoulder as she left, "Save me some lamb."

Rian looked at the cooks in the kitchen who stopped to

wait for his next direction. "Let's cook this critic a kick-ass dinner."

"I'M COMPLETELY STUFFED." Mara leaned back in her chair, putting her closer to Tiffany, who'd just received her dinner from Selena. "Did you like yours, Rachel?"

Rachel nodded. "Yes! I've never eaten lamb before, but I'm now in love with it." She shifted to the side and peered around Mara. "We need to come back next week, have it again before they take it off the menu." She mouthed her last word, "Phone."

Tiffany had taken three phone calls before her dinner arrived. Mara had tried to hear what she'd said but only grabbed at bits and pieces. She'd definitely been talking about O'Keeley's and seemed a little irritated at whoever continued to call.

This time, her voice rose louder. "It's great. Just like every other dish I've had here."

Wait. Mara sat up straight. If it was great, then why had she written such nasty things about Rian's food?

"No, Philip!" Tiffany's sharp voice cause Rachel's eyes to widen. "Philip, listen to me. Your food is great, too. You don't —" She sighed. "I get it. I know. I know."

Mara couldn't help herself. She hadn't seen the woman in question and risked getting caught eavesdropping to put a face with her voice. She dropped her napkin and bent to pick it up.

Dang. Tiffany was beautiful. Pale blonde hair and fair skin. Close to forty-five or fifty. She crossed her legs, bouncing her foot and shaking her head at whatever Philip said to her.

"I can't write that. No. Honey, listen—"

Honestly, Philip sounded like an asshole. Mara wanted to turn around, invite Tiffany to their table, so she could bond with her by complaining about her ex, Shane.

"Fine. Yes. You're right."

No, Tiffany, hold strong!

"Alright. Yeah. Bye." Tiffany's cell phone sounded like a brick hitting the table.

Mara's need to comfort another woman in a shitty relationship overrode her hesitancy. Being raised in the deep South gave her the ultimate conflicting personality traits.

First, the overwhelming need to help a stranger.

Second, the knowledge that she needed to mind her own business.

Well, three traits, because when she threw in her need for gossip, it was a coin toss as to how she'd react.

Mara shifted in her seat and made eye contact. "Are you alright?" Mara truly meant the question. She wasn't reaching out as a snoop for Rian. The woman sounded like she either needed a way out from Philip or at least someone to vent to.

Tiffany blinked. "I'm fine. Why do you ask?"

Mara shrugged, the *mind your own business* trait hating her. "You sounded upset, and you're alone. I felt compelled to ask."

Tiffany's shoulders relaxed a fraction. "I'm fine. Really. Thanks, though." Her leg bouncing resumed. "Tell me, did you enjoy your meal?"

"Loved it." The honest truth.

"I did, too," Rachel added. "Do you like yours?"

She slouched. "Yes." She poked her fork at the small amount of lamb left on her plate. "That's the problem."

"Did you not want to like it?" Mara cocked her head to

the side, giving her a crazy look. "I'm not sure I'd come here hoping to hate the food. Seems like a waste of money. And effort."

"It'd make it easier if I didn't like it." She leaned forward. "Have you ever dated a guy that changes who you are, but you don't see a way out?"

"Yes."

"Absolutely," Rachel agreed. "But she definitely has. What was your ex's name? Big Shane?"

Tiffany's lips twitched. "Big Shane?"

Mara rolled her eyes. "That wasn't my nickname for him. Believe me."

Tiffany giggled. She didn't feel like the enemy in the situation any longer.

"He was into weightlifting." Mara rested her arm on the back of the chair. "I became a different person with him. Or, really, I was the same person but weak. I let him push me around. Dictate everything I did. What I wore. What I ate. Made me feel bad that I couldn't lose weight." Mara picked up her wine and took a sip. "I finally left him, but I had to leave my hometown to get away. My family still loves him and never really understood. They never saw the shouting and insults, and I didn't want to tell them. We were supposed to get married."

Tiffany's foot bouncing resumed. "Philip raises his voice, but only when he's frustrated. I don't feel like myself right now." She picked up her wine glass and frowned that it was empty.

Mara spotted Selena on the other side of the restaurant, watching them with a curious expression. Talking to the enemy wasn't part of the deal. Mara's life was in social services. When she saw someone that needed to vent, work out their problems, she jumped in feet first.

She motioned for Selena.

Selena came immediately. "Yes?" She looked between Tiffany and Mara.

"She needs more wine, please." Mara smiled at Tiffany.

Tiffany shook her head. "I really shouldn't—"

"Look," Mara began. "I had the ultimate asshole boyfriend, and I think you need to vent and get it out of your system. It will help clear things up either way."

Tiffany smiled. "Are you a psychologist?"

"My degree is in psychology. Right now, I work with inner-city kids. Butting into their lives is kinda my job."

"Alright, then." She held up her glass. "One more glass in honor of the asshole. It might help to get it off my chest."

"Absolutely." Selena looked at the three women. "In honor of the jerk I dated in my twenties, I'm also bringing three free desserts."

Rachel stood up and pulled her chair over beside Mara. "I'm ready. Spill it, sister."

8

"What the hell is happening out there?" Rian paced back and forth in Brogan's office. The critic had been there for two hours, chatting away with Mara and Rachel like she was their long-lost best friend. He'd never tried to understand women and didn't want to figure them out now. He just wanted the critic to write a decent review and have Mara beside him.

And he wasn't sure which one he wanted more at the moment.

Cathal's voice came over speakerphone on Rian's cell phone he'd set on the desk. "Well, it appears to have turned into a male-bashing contest, according to our Selena. Who, by the way, egged them on by giving them free desserts and more wine."

"I can't get Mara to go have a drink with me, but she'll offer a stranger a shoulder to cry on?" Rian tossed his baseball hat to the other side of the room. "And it's my name on the line!"

"Calm down. I could hear that shout out here at the bar. You should have let me hit on Rachel when I offered instead of feeding me until my gut hurt. Oh. They seem to be done. Tiffany is leaving. Do you want me to go hit on Rachel now?"

"No!"

"Since when are you the angry one of the three of us?" Cathal chuckled. "Your Mara is glancing around the restaurant; I assume looking for you. Tiffany gave them both a hug and—" he paused "—now she's gone. Do you want me to bring Mara to the office?"

"Yes." Rian ended the call and continued his pacing.

The door opened. Brogan and Selena walked in, holding hands like everything was bloody sunshine and roses. Glad no one else felt his stress level. No one else had their confidence shaken. First with his food and second with Mara.

Cathal's laugh floated into the office a moment before Mara appeared in the doorway.

Rian shoved his hands in his pocket to keep from snatching her to his chest and kissing her. That wasn't who he was. He held a steady grip over his emotions. That included his attraction. The stress of the food critic must have him on edge or something.

"How did it go?" Selena asked, motioning Mara to come into the office. Rachel followed right behind, her eyes locked on Cathal. Well, he'd tried to keep them apart.

"We figured out the reason for the bad reviews," Mara said.

Rian crossed his arms, straightening his shoulders. He could take the criticism. "My food?"

Her eyes traced down his body and then back up in one quick look. Her lips tilted on one side like he amused her. "Do you know a Philip Tremaine?"

"The Canadian chef?"

"Bingo. That's her boyfriend. He's been pressuring her to write reviews for various restaurants around town."

Dropping out of English, he focused on Cathal. "That stupid piece of shit—" was how Rian started, letting the descriptive and rude insults on Philip fly in French and releasing his frustration.

Until Mara's wide-eyed, shocked expression.

He hung his head. "You speak French. I forgot."

"Hell," Cathal muttered. "You really need some help with women. And I thought Brogan was the lost cause."

Brogan grinned and tightened his hold on Selena.

Mara's hand rested on Rian's forearm. He lifted his eyes to meet hers. "I'm sorry for my language, Mara."

"If it makes you feel better, I only recognized like three words." She smiled. "Although, I might have to get you to teach me the rest of it. My formal French training didn't include those kinds of phrases."

"I'll have to remember to use Dutch next time."

Mara tilted her chin up. "I speak Dutch, too."

"Seriously?"

She laughed. "No. You should've seen your face, though." She squeezed his arm. "But the Philip situation explains why everyone else in the world thinks your restaurant is amazing, and only Tiffany finds it bad. She absolutely loved the lamb."

"Does this mean she'll write an honest review?" Selena asked. She smiled at Brogan when he handed her a glass of water.

Mara winced. "I don't think so." She looked back over to Rachel.

"I'd hope she won't be as nasty as before, but—" Rachel paused and lifted a shoulder.

"There's no telling. She's not in a good relationship right

now. I feel terrible for her." Mara's hand lingered on his skin, her thumb brushing back and forth and creating a small trail of warmth in its path. "But I know it's hurting your name in the process. We actually tried to get her to dump the guy."

"Philip is a domineering bastard." Rian patted her hand and moved away to keep from hauling her to her toes and kissing her. "I appreciate what you did."

"I'd lie if I said I did it for you. She needed a friend. You could tell by the way she talked to him on the phone it was a bad relationship when she spoke about your food."

"What did she say?" Brogan asked.

Mara crossed her arms. "She flat out told Philip your food was amazing, just like every other time she came here. Does he have a competing restaurant or something?"

Rian poured himself a glass of Cathal's whiskey. At the last second, he poured one for Mara. He'd get his drink with her, even in the company of four other people.

He held up the glass. "Rachel's driving, right?"

Rachel spoke for her. "Yes, I am. Drink up, Amara."

"Amara? I didn't realize that was your name. That's so pretty." Selena smiled. "I'm mentally collecting baby names at the moment. It's amazing that until you're pregnant, you don't actually pay attention."

"Thank you." Taking the glass, Mara eyed the amber liquid. "And thanks for this."

"Philip does have a restaurant in Atlanta. Although, I suspect he is there about as often as I am. He travels around, too. He's not someone I'm friendly with."

Mara sipped the whiskey and wrinkled her nose. "Phew, that's strong." She shook her head like it might help with the flavor. "Based on how determined Philip seems, I assumed the two of you weren't besties?"

"I'm not sure I know what that is."

"Best friends," Mara added.

"Hate is a strong word to describe our relationship but fitting. We're competitors. Until this, I always assumed we fed off one another, pushing to be the better chef. But now —" Rian shrugged and downed half his glass of expensive whiskey. "Now it's personal."

Rachel laughed and leaned against the door frame. "Are you going to call him out and fight? I feel like this is the chef version of that fight scene in *Anchorman*."

Cathal smirked. "I would pay a thousand dollars to see that. I don't know what Philip looks like, but I'd put my wager on Rian there."

"As long as your brother didn't get hurt, right?" Rachel asked.

Rian looked to Brogan and then finished the last of his whiskey. Being the middle brother usually made him the peacemaker, although he'd fought when he was younger.

Brogan rarely fought. It wasn't in his personality. Cathal used to fight as much for the enjoyment of it as the necessity. Currently, his only trigger focused on women, like everything else his younger brother's world centered around.

Mara sipped her drink, grimacing again.

He smiled. "I can get you something else."

She shook her head. "No. I should head home anyway." She smiled at Selena and Brogan. "I really enjoyed it. If you ever want to feed people free food—" she hitched a thumb over her shoulder at Rachel "—we're your women."

Selena laughed. "We really appreciate you helping us out. We'll see you later, I'm sure."

"Bye," Rachel called from the door, her eyes locked on Cathal. "Do you want to go out later?"

Cathal winced and rubbed his hand over his heart. "You don't know how much it pains me to say that I traded my chance with you for a plate of lamb earlier this evening."

Rian pinched the bridge of his nose. His brother didn't have any damn sense.

But Rachel only laughed. "I don't know whether to be offended or flattered because the lamb was delicious. *If* you change your mind, I might be at the tequila bar down the road later. C'mon, Mara."

Mara watched Rian for a long second. "Thank you for the drink."

"You're welcome. I'd like to take you out sometime, on a proper date." He ignored his audience. His brothers would have given him hell for *not* asking her out. "Tuesday."

She took so long to answer; he figured she tried to think of a reason to decline.

"Okay."

"Promise?"

She nodded and followed Rachel out the door.

He'd do everything in the world to make sure she kept her word. He'd never been so set on one woman the way he was on Mara.

"Good job, Rian." Selena sat down on the sofa beside Brogan. "All three of y'all have completely different approaches to dating women. It's interesting to watch."

Cathal plopped down in the chair and propped his feet on the coffee table. "What are my brothers' styles? I figure they're just lucky bastards as you and Mara seem to have better sense than to cave in."

"Rian is smooth. Quiet. Forceful. Similar to how he is in general. You have so much confidence, Rian, you don't expect a woman to push back. The tall, silent type."

Selena pegged him, except when they did push back as Mara did, he was at a loss as to what to do about it.

Cathal nodded. "I see that. What about your husband? How did Brog win you over? Was it the time he hid you in the bathroom?"

"Or shoved you under a desk?" Rian asked.

Selena smiled sweetly while Brogan glowered at his brothers. Served him right for treating his wife that way.

"No. Brogan's a caretaker." She patted his knee. "He's a tender, considerate person with a straight caveman underneath." She winked at Cathal. "The caveman won me over in the end."

"And me, darling. What is my style?" Cathal motioned to his brothers. "I'm not the silent type, and I'm definitely not the tender caveman."

"According to Fiona at the bar, you like to badger your women to death." Rian smirked at his brother's inappropriate gesture.

Selena leaned forward. "You charm them blind. You know exactly what to say, how to say it. You know when to touch them, how to touch them. And when to exit stage left without breaking their heart." She clasped her hands together and tilted her head to the side, analyzing him. "I'm just wondering when one of them will break yours."

Cathal shifted in his seat and glanced toward Rian. "No. Rian and I are the same in that regard. You picked the only O'Keeley that wants the family, late nights by the fire with a pretty woman. Permanency."

"And you don't?" She looked between him and Rian. "Ever?"

Brogan touched her knee. "Leave it, Selena."

She pressed her lips together in a thin line and shifted back against Brogan. "I don't believe it."

"Believe it, dear sister." Rian crossed his arms and leaned his hip against the desk. "You heard my story. I don't want that again. Ever." He nodded toward Cathal. "His story puts him in a similar mindset."

"But—"

"Selena." Brogan's deep voice wasn't loud, but it made her pause.

"Fine. Fine. I'll drop it. I just hate to see you cut yourself off from what you could have with Mara. She's smart. Caring. Pretty."

"And probably wants a family. A house. A man that will come home every night. That's not me. And I don't want to be that. Not even for Mara." He glanced at his watch. "I'm going to head home. Any more whiskey and Cathal might talk me into going out for the night, and right now, I need to go home and brood. Consider what I'm going to do about Philip."

He pushed off Brogan's desk and left. He didn't want to answer the questions in Selena's eyes. He'd given her the only answer he had. He didn't want that type of permanence in his life. He wasn't opposed to having a relationship with a woman that lasted longer than a night. It'd be new, but not scary. Not when he thought of that woman being Mara.

He'd offered her one night last time. He knew she wasn't that type. So he wouldn't treat her like that type. He'd date her. Casually. And see where things might lead.

9

Walking along the sidewalk in Atlanta in early fall typically relaxed her. A few cars drove past, but, otherwise, Mara was alone as she approached O'Keeley's. With the temperatures cooling as the sun began to set, she slipped her hands into her light jacket and tried not to think of the one-trillion ways that she could screw this up with Rian.

Mara's nerves made her steps feel stiff and heavy. She'd agreed to meet him at O'Keeley's on Tuesday at eight. He'd wanted to pick her up, insisted on it, but that meant he'd drop her off. At her apartment. Near the bed where, for the past four nights, she'd dreamed of him.

She wanted him there, even though she'd never permit herself to take what she wanted, what he'd offered. One night. She couldn't have stopped being a damn prude for one night in her life.

"Hello." He stepped out of the front door of his restaurant. "You look beautiful." Without pausing, he leaned down and kissed her cheek like it was an everyday occurrence.

Like he didn't know it caused her entire body to flush despite the chilly night.

"Hi." She unzipped her jacket to let out some of the built-up steam. The *last* thing she needed to do was sweat on this date. "Where are we going for dinner?" She motioned to her clothes, dark jeans, and a green blouse. "I hope I dressed alright. I wasn't sure how upscale you were planning."

"It's casual. I assure you." He reached for her hand, interlacing his fingers with hers. Now she really needed to take her jacket off, but she suffered in silence. They turned the corner into the employee parking lot behind O'Keeley's. "Where did you park?"

"In that deck down the street. It's free after six."

"It's open twenty-four hours, too, so you don't have a curfew."

"Yeah, but I do have work tomorrow."

"Of course. Right."

He made it sound like he didn't believe it.

He unlocked his car. Black and sleek. A two-seater that didn't even have room in the back for another person. "In you go." He opened her door.

"This is nice."

"Thanks." He closed her door and took long steps to his side before she could figure out the seat belt.

"You didn't say where we were going. I assumed we'd go to Philip's restaurant and try to scope it out."

"He'd recognize me if he's there." Rian grinned. "Although I may send you and Rachel in there undercover."

She held her hands up. "I assure you we are up for free dinners anywhere you want to send us. Fancy restaurants. Fast food. Gas stations."

He laughed. "Good to know you have a discerning palate."

"Seriously, though, where are we going?"

"My apartment. I'm cooking for you."

And that was the last thing she needed. The nearly perfect man just amped up his game. Cooking for her? Seriously? That happened in Hallmark movies. If he dressed up as Santa each year for the retirement home, took in stray dogs, and chopped down his own Christmas tree, she'd run screaming from his condo. No one was *that* perfect.

He pulled up to the valet in front of his condominium. She'd passed by his building dozens of times before, wondering who lived there. If the car hadn't proved Rian's wealth, the prices on the condos did. He held her hand, winked, and led her to the elevator as if her being here with him was the most natural thing in the world.

She almost stopped at the doorman and asked if Rian did this often. She hated to be petty, but if she was number four hundred and thirty-two on his list of women, she wanted to know that going into this dinner.

They arrived on the seventeenth floor, barely having said two words. With the way her palms sweated, opting to keep quiet beat running her mouth non-stop, which was her usual M.O. when she was nervous. Small town girls from rural Alabama knew when they were out of their league.

Besides, Rian didn't strike her as a chatty man. Not like his brother Cathal, who, even though he'd taken the lamb over Rachel, might have met up with her friend later that night. Rachel had eluded to having partaken in a rendezvous with the youngest O'Keeley but wouldn't divulge any details. And, frankly, Mara didn't want them.

He opened his door and motioned her inside. "Here we

are." He followed her in and closed the door. "Make yourself at home."

She stood in the middle of the foyer, surveying his space. Calling his condo a "home" was a stretch. Nothing in there was cozy or friendly. Instead, it was empty. Sparse. He was warmer than his decorating skills indicated. Was that part of why he seemed to roam around so much? She'd researched him, confirmed he traveled as much as he claimed. But why? Just for his job?

She slipped off her jacket. Now was not the time to psychoanalyze her date.

A hazard of her job. Backgrounds and environments held a direct correlation on someone's actions and personality. The juxtaposition for Rian was extreme. How did the man that took her coat, kissed her neck, and just called her something in one of the half-dozen languages he knew be the same man who enjoyed living in a room that made the dentist office look homey?

A first date wasn't the time to get into someone's background. She had plenty of her own issues she still contended with that she'd rather not ever reveal to Rian. He looked so put together—nothing like the mess that Shane had left of her heart.

"Wine?" He held up a bottle.

"Sure. I assume you pick your wine to go with your meal?"

He looked at the label. "Yes. But not this one. This one I picked to enjoy before the meal. I found out the type of wine you ordered at O'Keeley's and went from there."

"What is that?"

"A red Bordeaux."

She sat at the counter, trying to relax. "Do you know wine like you do food?"

"I know what I want to go with my meal. Otherwise," he paused and held up his phone. "I have a few friends I can ask."

Admitting to not knowing everything eased her mind a little. She set her hands on the counter instead of gripped in her lap. Relax. He was the same man as before.

His eyes, green in the soft light, watched her. That didn't unnerve her at all.

She smiled, hoping to break the spell he seemed to drag her under. "So, tell me about Ireland."

His grin was quick as he popped the cork out of the wine bottle. "Do you want a full history of the country or a shortened version?"

She shook her head and laughed. "You know what I mean. Tell me about when you lived there."

"We lived in Roscommon. My family had a farm." He poured a glass and held it out to her. "Taste this."

She recognized the avoidance tactic, done it plenty of times herself when it came to the details as to why she'd left Alabama. Minimal information and change the topic. She wouldn't push him on divulging his past. His accent sounded as though he might try to smooth it out. Especially compared to Cathal's sound.

She sipped the wine. "Oh. Wow. That's wonderful." She eyed the bottle. "I'm guessing it's not sold in the local grocery store."

"No, it's not." He poured himself a glass and turned to the fridge. "Are you adventurous with your food, Amara?"

With the way he said her full name, she wished she never had the nickname. It sounded pretty in his accent. Exotic. "I think I'm up for whatever you plan to cook."

"We have two options. I have salmon, or we can order pizza."

"Pizza?" She held up her wine. "With this?"

He reached into the fridge and pulled out a Bud Lite. "I planned for both."

Did he do this for all his dates? Wine and dine them this way? Be this considerate? It was hard not to picture who else might have been with him, in his condo, before.

But she couldn't let herself go down that road. At their age, they both would have had multiple partners. Well, he did. She was still at one and a half. One for Shane. The half for a guy she dated for six months that she couldn't even remember his last name at the moment.

"Salmon is fine." She scanned his apartment again. "You don't have any pictures. At all."

He pulled out a tray with the salmon and set out some vegetables from the bin on the counter. "No. I'm not here enough to worry about that. I bought this condo, asked a decorator to put in the essentials, and this is what we have." He started prepping the fish. "Did you want to help me?" He glanced over his shoulder. "What do you typically cook for dinner?'

She slipped out of the barstool and walked to stand beside him. "Not salmon."

"Fish is fairly easy. So, what is it? Chicken? Steak?"

"You really don't want to know."

He bumped his shoulder with hers. "It can't be that bad. Will you hand me that salt grinder?"

She passed it to him. He chopped the vegetables with quick, precise movements. His hands were pretty. Strong. She'd never thought about that before for a man.

And he'd confirmed that she sure as hell would never cook in front of the man at her apartment. She owned one sharp knife that she used for everything and calling it sharp was a stretch. In fact, when she did try to cook, she avoided the knives and used a pair of kitchen scissors. If she couldn't cut it with scissors, it wasn't getting chopped.

She reached over and picked up her wine, wanting to savor each drop and at the same time chug it so she'd loosen up already. She typically stayed sober on dates. It was her thing. One maybe two glasses of beer or wine and done.

But Rian was different.

He was made to be on the cover of a magazine. No matter how many times she saw him, the full force of his good looks never wore off. Would it ever? Did people in long-term relationships with gorgeous men and women ever lose that state of shock?

"I'm serious. What do you cook? I'm on this mission to try and fuse my own cooking with American cuisine. You said you grew up in Alabama, right? I'm sure you have some good recipes." He stopped working and lifted his head. "Unless it's as weird as it sounds that I want to swap recipes with my date like I'm an eighty-year-old woman."

"Maybe just a little. Besides, you don't want to swap recipes with me. I can tell you the best frozen meals to buy, though. Finding a good country fried steak is hard."

His hands stalled. He canted his head to the side and looked at her like she might turn into a monster any second. His mouth opened, probably to denounce her as some spawn of Satan, but it snapped closed immediately.

"That's fine, then. Just fine." He slowly nodded. "*Can* you cook?"

"My mom thinks I can."

"Your mom cooks?" The hope in his eyes nearly made her laugh.

She patted him on the shoulder. "Yes. And she taught me to cook. I just choose not to. I'd much rather let someone else cook, be it the frozen food gods or you."

He reached out and captured her waist, tugging her to stand in front of him. "I'd much rather be the one to cook for you." He slipped his hand along her cheek and cradled the back of her head. "Amara..."

He leaned down and kissed her.

This time, she prepared herself for the shock that zipped through her body. The sudden urge to throw caution to the wind, to flat out ask him where his bedroom was, demanding a second chance on the one-night deal.

His bodyweight pinned her hips to the counter. He liked that position of power. Control. The psychologist in her tried to emerge and analyze him again, but she just heard herself moan as his lips trailed down her throat.

"Is this part of the cooking process I've missed out on?"

He smiled against her skin. "It's the appetizer."

She barked out a laugh.

He raised his head, still smiling. "That cheesy, huh?"

"Absolutely," she said in between laughs. Managing to get herself under control, she fisted her hands in his T-shirt and pulled him back down to kiss him again. She slid her hands down his chest and rested on his waist. She shouldn't feel so greedy to want to touch him.

He'd invited her to his bed, and she'd declined.

And now, all she wanted to do was get her hands on him. So, she did. She slipped her hands underneath the edge of his shirt and felt his warm skin. Her fingers grazed over defined muscles that were more subtle than Shane's.

No. Don't even bring that jackass into this moment. She was with Rian. Wanted to be with Rian. Shane was in the past. She didn't suspect she had much of a future with Rian, but she'd take living in the present.

Her phone rang, a loud, shrill sound that only indicated one person could be calling.

"Do you need to get it?" He pressed a kiss to a spot behind her ear. "God, every time I catch that sweet scent of peaches on your skin, I think of dessert."

She looked at the ceiling, wishing dessert was on the menu. "I'll have to answer it eventually. She won't stop calling until I do." She moved away, feeling a chill from where she'd been pressed against him.

"Who? Rachel?"

She held up her phone. "Nope. My mom." The ultimate date destroyer.

10

The parking lot for the after-school program where she worked wasn't too far from O'Keeley's. He'd passed by it before he knew Mara and never thought twice. This time, when he drove past it, he pulled in. She'd arrive at work in the next fifteen minutes, he figured. It was Thursday, and he'd not seen Mara since Tuesday night. They'd not set another date, and that bothered him.

Their date at his apartment had been perfect, up until her ma called.

After that, Mara had kept her distance, cleaned her plate, finished her wine, and he'd driven her back to her car. She'd seemed happy but distracted by whatever her ma had told her.

He hated that. Not for him, although he wished he could have had another long taste of her. She needed a break from work and the kids at the center. He wanted to be the one to give it to her.

To give her a break from the damn frozen dinners she ate every night.

But he could do something. She'd mentioned going back to Alabama for the weekend.

Rian leaned against his car, waiting on her to arrive. He'd already sent four of the boys he'd played dodge ball with inside after they crawled through his Mercedes. He would have done the same thing at their age, seeing a sports car.

Her tidy car pulled in beside his, and he was greeted with a bright smile. "Hello," she called, stepping out and setting her purse strap over her shoulder. "This is a surprise."

"I wanted to see you before you left tomorrow." He didn't question the meaning behind his need to see her. He'd established he could have a more committed relationship with Mara and it not lead to marriage and a family. He'd have to start traveling again, anyway.

She smiled. "That's sweet of you."

"You sound as though that shocks you."

Her eyes widened. "No. Not at all, I'm just not used to it. You're, well, you. And I'm me. I'm not sure I'll ever get used to it."

Several women had thrown themselves his direction in the past because of his fame. Now, the woman he wanted was hesitant.

"I'm no different than any other man that wanted to date you."

She tapped him on the shoulder. "Ah. There's the problem. No other man wants to date me."

"Then they're idiots, and I'm glad for it."

She twisted her lips to the side. "A glass-half-full viewpoint. There's always the option that maybe, the glass *is* half-empty, and you're the odd one out."

He couldn't stand her thinking she wasn't whatever she thought she needed to be to date him. Consistently dating one woman wasn't even in his life until Amara. He wouldn't tell her that. Then he'd have to explain why.

He stepped to her, slipping his hand along her waist and resting it on her lower back. "Amara, I'm here with you at the moment. And I think you should kiss me."

Her eyes widened. "Here?"

"Yes." He kissed her. Like he needed to prove something to her. Show her he wanted her like a man wants a woman. More than that, though. He glided his hands from her hips to her waist and back down. Every tabloid newspaper linked him with models. Sure, he'd dated a few, but this, a woman under his hands, was what he loved.

Especially knowing that woman was Mara. He never experienced the attraction to a woman he genuinely cared about.

She turned her head to the side, breaking the kiss. "Rian." Her breathless voice, hands tightly holding onto his arms, made his mouth run dry. "We can't do this here."

"Then come home with me tonight. I know you need to leave for your parents' tomorrow—"

"Right. And you said you leave next week."

"Come stay with me, Mara." Again, he knew it was too soon. He could see that in her eyes, and he hated himself for even suggesting it. He backed away. "Sorry. I know that's not you." Wanting her so damn bad clouded his judgment.

"It's okay. Really. Every time I tell you 'no' I worry if I'm going to get another shot."

"It doesn't matter if it's a year from now, you will always have a shot." He ran a hand down her arm and linked his fingers with hers. "You jumped out of my car so fast, I never got to ask you why you're going?"

"Both my brothers are coming home to help rebuild the shed after that storm last week. Mom wants me there because she's having an impromptu family reunion. I told her I'd stay Friday and Saturday night."

"You know I grew up on a farm. I can help."

Her body froze. "But, you'll be working at O'Keeley's all weekend."

"I don't have to. I mean, the business runs just fine with me on the other side of the world. Brogan put me in charge of the kitchen. I hired competent people to be in charge of the kitchen." Was he seriously considering coming to her parents' house? He'd gone from never having an attachment, to convincing himself it was okay to have a small relationship with Amara, to offering to meet her da.

He must be deranged. And that was her fault.

"I don't know. My family is a little overwhelming at times."

"Have you met my brothers? Besides, we're related to half the damn county it seems back home. Large, loud families are in my blood. So is building. I can help. Really. And it will give me a chance to see you more before I leave Tuesday."

"How long will you be gone?"

"Ten days."

She frowned. Some women pouted to get their way. He'd seen that a dozen times. Mara's frown was genuine. "Ten days? That stinks."

He wrapped his arms around her shoulders and pulled her back to his chest. That peaches smell clung to her. "You're going to miss me, aren't you?"

Hesitantly, she slipped her arms around his waist. Much better. "I will miss you. And your cooking." At his fake indignation, she laughed. "Don't even. The meals at O'Keeley's and your apartment makes it hard to go back to my frozen meatloaf."

"That sounds incredibly unappetizing. I'm tempted to make you a dozen casseroles and freeze them for you to eat."

Her eyebrows wiggled. "Is that one of the perks of dating a chef?"

He leaned down, sinking into one more kiss from her. "There are several perks." He trailed a path of kisses along her neck. "You haven't taken advantage of the other ones yet."

Mara let her head drop to the side and she half-laughed. "I really shouldn't let you do this here."

"Oh, you really should." And more. As much as she was willing to give. "Let me come with you this weekend."

"We won't be able to do this at my parents' house."

He looked down at her. "Are you ashamed of me?" The idea amused him. He'd worked hard to have prestige. Money. Reputation.

"No. Not exactly. Let's just say that my family is still pretty much set on me marrying my ex-boyfriend. He'll probably be there. It's easier if we don't rock the boat."

"I think I can hold my own."

His answer seemed to please her for some reason. She shook her head. "Alright. Don't say I didn't warn you."

"I'll drive."

She glanced at his car. "Better let me. I don't want people to see your car and judge you negatively."

"Negatively? How is that possible? That car cost well over a hundred thousand dollars."

She brushed her lips along his cheek. "I know. And everyone will wonder why you feel the need to show off your money. I'll call my mom and tell her we'll come on Saturday morning. It's about a two-hour drive from here. We can leave around seven if that's okay? Stay through dinner?"

"That's fine with me." He let her step away. "You're

always welcome to stay over tonight. Or Friday night. Then we can leave from my place Saturday morning."

"Rian—"

"What about Saturday night?" He grinned and winked. "It'll be late when we get back."

Mara crossed her arms, looking like she tried not to smile. "You don't give up, do you?"

"Not when it's something I want." He opened his car door. "The wanting you won't change, Mara. It won't change tomorrow. It won't change in the ten days I'm gone."

"Uh-huh. I'll see you at seven on Saturday. I'll pick you up."

At least Mara knew the truth. He wouldn't give up. He'd want her the same in ten days as he did right then. Maybe by then, she'd be used to the idea.

MARA WALKED into the after-school program floating ten feet off the ground. She'd declined Rian, again, but her mind wasn't made up. For the first time, she seriously considered staying over Saturday night after they returned from Alabama. It was quick, at least for her, but it didn't feel wrong.

Everything about Rian felt right.

Too right.

The scary kind of right where she knew, at any moment, she'd wake up from whatever dream she was having. Or that Rian would change, shift into some egotistical maniac like Shane, and make her regret being with him.

She turned the corner and walked into the gym. Romeo, blood dripping down the front of his shirt, took a swing at another kid. Dropping her bag, Mara ran forward. She'd broken up several fights before, but none with a kid as strong as Romeo.

"Stop!" She pushed her way into the fight.

Romeo pulled up short of hitting her with a punch. His eyes widened. "Ms. Mara?"

"Stop it right now." She pointed at a bench along the side of the gym floor. Raising her voice over the kids' cheering them on, she said, "Go. Sit. Now."

"But you don't understand—"

"I'll deal with you in a second." She whirled around to get a look at who Romeo fought. He was a new guy who looked to be Romeo's age, fourteen, with light-colored eyes and a rich ebony skin tone. It was an unusual combination that, when combined with the murderous look he shot her, freaked her out a little bit.

"Jason, right?" She didn't wait for confirmation. That was the kid's name. "What happened?"

Jason wiped his mouth with the back of his hand, smearing the small trickle of blood across his skin. "Nothin' that concerns you."

Nothing. Of course, that would be the answer. "You're fighting, and I'm in charge, that does concern me."

Mrs. Peterson stormed from her office. Better late than never, Mara supposed.

"I've got it under control, Mrs. Peterson."

"You're late, Amara." She pointed at Romeo along the wall. "He's always causing trouble."

Mara stepped in between Romeo and Mrs. Peterson. "We can't jump to that conclusion. I haven't figured out who started the fight."

"It doesn't matter who started it. It matters that Romeo even participated. Why didn't he walk away? We've reminded him that he needs to tell an adult after the two fights he's had." Mrs. Peterson shifted to the side, able to see Romeo again. "I told his aunt the next fight I caught him in that he was out of the center."

Mara took a breath. Three weeks and this woman would be out of her life, and then she could run the center the best way she knew how.

"Romeo needs to be here." Mara raised an eyebrow at Jason's smirk. "I'm waiting to hear his explanation on the cause of the fight. Romeo knows the rules. He wouldn't get in a fight if it weren't something big."

"Big? Amara, there's never a reason for a fight." Mrs. Peterson shook her head and crossed her arms.

That woman never listened to reason. She didn't understand kids from these neighborhoods. Some fights were inevitable. Romeo needed this after school program. At-risk was an understatement for the kid. His mother died a few years ago. His father was a drug dealer who was out on probation. His aunt tried to shield him, but working two jobs made that difficult with a lack of supervision.

"He's out. Period. The end. That's it." Mrs. Peterson turned and stomped back across the floor to her office.

Mara braced for the tears. These kids wound themselves into her heart. But the tears never came. Anger. Resentment. Pity. She didn't have room or time to wallow in the consequences.

"Jason," she began, cutting her eyes at the boy. Yes, he definitely had a smile on his face. "You're kicked out of the after-school program for this semester."

The smile dropped. "What? He had like ten chances, she said. That was my first fight." Jason pointed at Romeo. "Man, this is some shit right here."

Mara held up her hand at the language. She took a step in his direction. "Watch it. Go. Sit. I'm calling your mom."

She pointed at a bench on the opposite side of the gym. If Romeo was out of the program, the other guy was out as well.

She crossed the gym. Sympathy for Romeo rammed through her. His angry stare broke her heart. No kid at fourteen should have so much aggression inside of them.

She squatted down in front of him and rested her hands on his knees. "Romeo, what happened?"

"It doesn't matter," he mumbled. "I'm out anyway."

"It does matter. To me. What happened?" She squeezed his knees. "Tell me."

He looked away. "Jason said somethin' about you."

She straightened up. "Me?"

"Yeah. He said he saw you out there with a guy. He called you a name I didn't like."

Rian. She closed her eyes. Their kiss had ended Romeo's time at the center. Rian wasn't to blame, she was. She should have tried harder to push him away instead of letting him kiss her that way. That wasn't even the reason she'd tried to stop. She'd been more worried about Mrs. Peterson seeing her than a kid.

"I don't want to know anything else, Romeo. Just know that this arrangement won't last long."

He cut his eyes at her. "What do you mean?"

"If I can somehow not screw things up, in three weeks, I'll be in Mrs. Peterson's position, and I'll enroll you in the program again." Strange, talking to a child about her job, but he'd seen more in life than she had.

"Really? But until then—" He looked away, staring at the other kids. "I'm out, right?"

"Yes." Her jaw hurt from clenching. Mrs. Peterson wouldn't change her mind. She knew that just by the stubborn set to the lady's chin. "But maybe I can find something else for you to do for the next few weeks. Somewhere else to go. I don't think your aunt will care."

"My aunt doesn't give a crap about me."

"That's not true." The woman did her best. "Let me think about it."

"What do I do tomorrow?"

Where could he go? Mara racked her brain. Part of her would let him go hang out at her apartment. Fourteen wasn't too young to be alone, but even though she loved Romeo, she still didn't trust him that much.

"Come here tomorrow, just like always. I'll see what I come up with."

11

Rian looked up from the table in the corner at O'Keeley's as Mara walked through the front door. At two in the afternoon, he'd not expected her, but it brought an unexpected jolt of happiness. Tomorrow they had their day trip to her parents' house.

He saved the recipe he'd just typed out, closed the lid of his laptop, and rose from his seat ready to greet her. It never got old, that punch to the gut when their eyes locked. It'd happened the first day they'd met and every time since.

She walked toward him, her lips set in a stern line. Was he in trouble? If she backed out of the trip to her parents' house tomorrow, he'd have a hard time hiding his disappointment. He needed that time with her.

"This is a nice surprise, although you don't look happy." He stepped to her.

She lifted her head to his, giving him a quick kiss that shot his system to life. "It's not a happy day. Something happened at the center yesterday."

"You could have called me last night."

She sat down at the table. "No. I didn't have a reason for

your involvement until an idea struck me today. I took off early to be here."

Ah. She missed his point. "You could have called me yesterday regardless."

She blinked. "Oh. Well. I will if you'd like."

He smiled, hoping to take away some of her confusion. "I enjoy hearing your voice." That admission made her grip her hands together in her lap. He liked the idea of talking to Mara every day. "What happened?"

She shifted forward, still looking nervous. "I have a *massive* favor to ask of you. Or Selena. I'm not sure who is in charge of O'Keeley's."

Rian threw his head back and laughed. "I wish my brother could hear that."

"What?"

He leaned across the table, planting another solid kiss on her lips. "That your choice for who was in charge of O'Keeley's rested between his Selena and me. Brogan has been in charge of everything since we left Ireland. It'd serve him right to know that someone in the world doesn't think he's the boss."

She chewed on her lip. "I don't want to upset your family."

"Darling, you won't be the reason we're upset. What is it?"

"Romeo was kicked out of the center for fighting."

The lightheartedness of the situation evaporated. "Really? Why'd he fight?" Romeo was a good kid. He'd seen the way Romeo helped Blair and encouraged the other guys but tried to sound tough at the same time. Deep down, the kid had a kind heart if he could make it through his teenage years and find a way in life.

"Because a new kid at the center saw us kissing in the

parking lot, and Romeo, it seems, defended my honor." She tilted her head to the side, her eyes focusing over his shoulder. "I'm responsible for it."

"No. I am. You asked me to stop." He crossed his arms, trying to keep from getting too angry at himself. It didn't matter where, if Mara was near him, he wanted, needed, to touch her. The reality of his obsession didn't sit well with him. But he didn't want to give it up. Not after it taking so long to *feel* that way about anyone again.

"Rian, neither one of us knew that would happen. That's not even what I was worried about when I said stop. I'm trying to get the position at the center when Mrs. Peterson leaves. She told me once already I wasn't allowed to see you since you were a volunteer."

He'd never agree that the kiss was Mara's fault. And she wanted that job. He knew it. Watching himself around her might prove difficult, but he wouldn't be the reason for her to lose out on her dream.

"Does she know why Romeo got into a fight?"

"No. And I won't tell her. Once I'm in charge, I'll bring Romeo back into the center. But for those three weeks, I don't have anywhere for him to go."

"And I assume his home life is unsuitable."

She huffed. "To say it politely, yes, it is." She chewed on her bottom lip and looked away, surveying the restaurant.

"You look as though you have a plan."

She exhaled between pursed lips. "Can he come here after school until then?" The question formed in a rush of words before she recoiled back into her seat.

"To O'Keeley's? What would he do here?"

She held her hands out. "I don't know. Anything. He could wash dishes. Sweep. Sit in a corner and read a book."

"Brogan would know before I would if a kid his age can work in America."

Mara nodded. "Yes, he can. He's fourteen. He can work three hours a day on school days. If he agrees to it."

"Who? Romeo or Brogan?"

She shrugged. "Both. I'm going out on a limb, I know. I'm asking for your entire family to do a favor for me. I'm sure the other women you've dated never had to ask for babysitting services."

No. Because until he'd met Mara, he never thought about things like that. The woman had such a caring heart. She probably wanted a house full of children. That was the number one reason he should terminate things immediately. Walk away. He wouldn't be the one to give them to her.

God, but he was selfish. For the moment, he'd take Mara and deal with the consequences later. She might hate him for it. That would just make the break-up easier for her in the end.

"Let me talk to Selena. When does he need to start?"

"Today."

"And his parents are alright with strangers watching him?"

For the first time since walking into the pub, she relaxed. "His aunt said she didn't care. And we'd get legal forms signed if he were actually to work here."

"Send him this way, then."

She shook her head slowly, a small smile making a tiny dimple next to her lips he'd never noticed before. "You're incredible."

"I'm not." He rose, uncomfortable with the praise. "I'm doing this solely to impress you."

She stood up and wrapped her arms around his waist. He liked her right there, tight against him.

"No, you're not, but I'll let you believe that."

She saw into his soul more than he liked. "Let me find my brothers and keep them in the loop. I know you're headed to the center."

"About tomorrow—"

He kissed her, ignoring the curious glances of the few tables with customers. If they held this woman in their arms, they wouldn't give a shit what other people thought either.

He ended the kiss with reluctance. "What about it? You're not backing out on me, are you?"

"No. I just—I just thought about what you said. About staying—afterward—at your place."

He cupped her cheek. Only if she was sure. "You can let me know on Saturday."

Her quick nod confirmed her nervousness. Was it him or being with any man? Who puts that uneasiness in her eyes? He kissed her forehead.

"I'll be on the lookout for Romeo."

"Thank you, Rian."

He hoped her decision Saturday night was based on her wants and not on her appreciation. Rian tilted her chin up and laid a light kiss on her lips.

"Let's be clear. I'm helping Romeo because he needs it. I don't need or want whatever takes place between us to be because you feel thankful."

She brushed her hand along his temple, seeming amused. "That's nice to hear. As much as I do like to show my appreciation for people who help out the underprivileged youth in the city, I don't usually do it in the form of sex. A 'thank you' card, usually suffices. Your willingness to give up afternoons to help a kid like Romeo is because you have a big heart." She leaned closer. "That is what makes me consider sleeping with you." She kissed him, giving him only a small taste of what he wanted. "Now, I do need to head out before I'm late. Can I stop by after work? See how it went?"

"Please do."

He let her leave his arms, standing in the same place until she left O'Keeley's. Things between them had shifted. It didn't scare him. Not yet. He never wanted to marry because he never wanted children.

Never chance that pain again.

"That was interesting." Selena walked up, her golden eyes bright and curious. "Things seem to be getting serious."

"Just the O'Keeley I wanted to see." Rian rested his arm around her shoulders. "How would you feel about helping out a kid that needs a place to hang out for a few weeks after school?"

She tilted her head back. "How little of a kid?"

"Fourteen."

"I don't guess I have a problem with it. Are we paying him to work or just letting him sit at a table?"

"His name is Romeo, and I think he'd do well to work. I worked at his age. So did Brogan. I'll hang around today. Mara said she can get the proper paperwork signed soon."

"What about next week when you're gone?"

"I might not be leaving after all. Plan on me being here with him until we get his work schedule settled if he's interested." Because for the first time, he didn't want to leave.

She snorted. "You? You're going to be at the restaurant every afternoon for *weeks*?"

"I'm considering it. Maybe, I'll pull him into the kitchen

with me. He was a good help at the center. Granted, he helped so he could be captain of a dodge ball team, but I'm sure we can find him some motivation." He liked the idea, watching over a kid like Romeo, helping push him to be his best.

"Let me give Brogan the heads up about it. And Cathal. And probably your kitchen staff. I feel like the world needs to know if you'll be stationary for weeks at a time."

"That's a little extreme." Rian glanced at the entrance. "Before you announce it to the world, go use your persuasive powers to make Brogan agree. The kid just showed up."

Romeo came in. He glanced around, trying to look like he knew what he was doing, but the relief was evident when his gaze landed on Rian.

Rian had grown up in a loving home, never needing any of the basics, but he understood that feeling of faking confidence. If people in the world suspected even the smallest weakness, they'd take advantage of it. The culinary world was cutthroat to a certain degree. Philip had proved that with his manipulation of Tiffany MacKnight and the horrible food reviews.

Selena, taking charge, walked ahead of Rian to where Romeo stood near the entrance. She held out her hand. "Hi, Romeo, I'm Selena."

He took her hand, looked away, and mumbled something.

Selena didn't seem phased. "I'm the person you'll come to if you need anything."

Romeo shoved his hands in his pockets. "Are you the boss?"

She smiled. "I'm married to the boss, which means I'm the boss's boss."

Romeo almost cracked a smile.

Rian did what he'd always done before, he faked knowing what to say. "So, do you have homework you need to do?"

"Yeah. A little bit." He shouldered his book bag. "I hate it."

"I did, too," Selena said.

"Me, too." Rian tried not to laugh at Romeo's shocked look. No one enjoyed homework. "You can sit at a table back there if you'd like. Are you hungry?"

Romeo grinned. "Absolutely."

"I'll bring you something out. Once you get done with homework, come to the kitchen. I'll teach you how to cook with only three ingredients."

"Three?" He raised his eyebrows. "I'm not sure you can do that, and it still tastes good."

"I guess you need to get done with that homework so you can find out." He patted Romeo on the shoulder and left him with Selena. Now, he just had to figure out what kids ate after school. He doubted Romeo would be as pleased as Cathal always was with a chunk of cold lamb to eat.

12

————

Walking into O'Keeley's with the plan to sleep with one of the owners gave Mara a little more confidence than usual. Even though it'd been a crappy day dealing with the fallout from Romeo and hoping her boss didn't hear the reason for the fight, seeing Rian pushed it all away. She tried to take the swagger out of her stride, but it refused to budge. Especially when the three O'Keeley men turned from the bar to watch her walk toward them.

They wore identical scowls that didn't change their attractiveness in the least. Even Cathal looked solemn. It gave him an angsty look that didn't fit with his personality but would make most women follow him around, hoping to be the one to restore him to his usual, jovial self. She wouldn't mention the effect to Rachel. Her friend had become obsessed with the youngest brother.

Mara didn't have to ask why they looked like three men planning the next move in a war.

Tiffany's review came out that afternoon after she'd left Rian to go to work.

And it wasn't the best.

Mara still sympathized with the woman. She had firsthand experience of losing yourself when dating a guy. And, after all the tears and self-doubt caused by Shane, she'd found Rian.

"Romeo just left," Rian said, holding out his arm.

She glided to his side. They fit together. And based on the tight look in his eyes, he needed support. That always brought up the questions in her mind about what they were or how long they'd last, but she ignored the uncertainty. He needed her. That was all that mattered.

Rising on her toes, she kissed his lips. "I want to hear how today went with Romeo, but I saw the review."

"All of Atlanta saw that damn review," Brogan grumbled from the end of the bar. He held a beer. Actually, they were all drinking beer.

"No whiskey?"

Brogan crossed his arms, looking big and intimidating and the complete opposite of his wife. "Whiskey isn't the drink necessary when you're devising a plan."

Cathal took a reluctant drink of his beer. "Speak for yourself."

"A plan for what?" Mara asked.

Rian set one hand on the bar, keeping the other firmly around her waist. "Figuring out what to do about the review."

Mara picked up Rian's beer and took a sip. Much better than drinking whiskey.

Brogan shifted on the stool, facing her. "We think Rian should call Philip on his shit and offer to hold a competition. Let impartial judges decide who's the best chef."

She looked up at Rian. "Like those *Iron Chef* competitions on TV?"

He took his beer back. "Not hardly."

Cathal walked around the bar, pulling out a new beer, taking the top off, and sliding it to Mara. "Rian would kick his ass. I've eaten at Philip's restaurant. There's a reason we beat them on every travel website for Atlanta." Cathal grinned. "And it's not just because we have a killer VP of Advertising."

Brogan muttered something that made Cathal laugh.

Rian tightened his fingers on Mara's hip, bringing her closer to his body.

She took a long drink of the cold beer, wishing she knew where their relationship was headed. Rian would leave next week. And probably the next month. And next year. Would he ever stop traveling?

Where did that leave her?

"What do you think, Mara?" Cathal leaned on the bar, watching her with a playful expression. "Do you have confidence that our Rian would win a culinary throw down?"

"Of course. I don't date losers."

All three brothers laughed. Rian kissed her temple again. "Then I guess I'm issuing Philip a challenge. But what will the prize be?"

"Personal glory?" Brogan offered.

"Pride is something you are fond of, brother," Cathal said.

"I think you should make Philip issue a public endorsement for our restaurant." Brogan motioned around the room. "Make him eat his words that he's forced Tiffany to write."

Rian tilted his head to the side. "If I were to lose under those conditions, I might end my association with O'Keeley's and retire to a remote island somewhere before I endorsed his piece of shit restaurant. I can't even fathom having to utter those words."

"But, you won't lose." Mara tilted back, studying his serious profile. "I think you know that deep down."

He leaned down, kissing her on the spot behind her ear she loved, whispering, "you have that much faith in me?"

She nodded. Of course, she did.

"What will you make?" Cathal knocked on the wooden bar, interrupting. "My vote is for the lamb again."

Rian cringed. "No. Not the damn lamb. It needs to be something different. Something I've never cooked." He squeezed Mara's shoulders. "What do you think?"

"Me?" She didn't have a clue what he could do.

He shifted her to stand in front of him, her back against the bar.

"Tell me, Amara, what do you like to eat? Fish? Chicken? Steak? If you could choose your last meal, what would it be?"

They were in the middle of the restaurant, dinner time and busy on a Friday night, and he looked at her with those eyes, the same way he did before he kissed her. She could flirt back a little, take away the feeling like it was a one-sided relationship where Rian made all the moves.

She stood up, forcing him to take a step back, but she didn't release his waist. Tilting her head to the side, she studied him for another long second. "I like dessert."

"I'll have to find something creative to cook for you, then." He leaned down, kissing her slow enough to make the burn come to life, before pulling away. He looked over her head. "Don't you have something better to do?"

She glanced over her shoulder. Cathal, chin propped in his hand, watched them. "Nope."

Rian pulled her away from the bar and toward the office. "Come along, Mara. I apologize for my brother."

She laughed. "No need. I think he's funny."

"That's about all he's good for. A laugh." He continued to pull her toward the back of the restaurant. Once she stepped into the office, he closed the door.

And locked it.

"Is that necessary?" She crossed her arms. Ten seconds ago, she had all the confidence in the world. That'd disappeared with the prospect of having to live up to what her flirting insinuated.

Rian leaned back against the door. "Yes. My brothers and other members of the staff don't see a closed door as a reason to slow down." He smiled, slow and sexy. "Did we want to discuss the dessert you mentioned?"

"Now?" She stepped farther into the office. Just like before, the room felt masculine. Tan walls. Leather sofas and chairs around an electric fireplace. A large, oak desk sat in the middle of the room with a chair on either side.

"Then we can talk about Romeo," Rian said. He crossed his arms. "After spending the afternoon with him, I think he needs to start working here officially. The kid's nice, despite his hard shell. He puts that up because otherwise, society will eat him alive. He needs the defense. We had one moment, about five minutes after he stepped into my kitchen, where I *kindly* explained how this will run while he's here. After that, no issues."

"Really? After one afternoon, you're willing to give him a chance like that?" She loved Romeo like a little brother, but he could be difficult. Stubborn. He did put up that defense, as Rian called it because it was necessary. Maybe getting kicked out of the center temporarily would be for the best.

"I knew after the first hour he needed to be working.

Actually, Selena sat and had a long conversation with him. Apparently, she grew up near where he lives. Romeo seems to trust her. She offered him the job; gave him an application to fill out. There are a few other steps to take with the State because of his age, but he seemed excited."

"And what about when you leave?"

His expression turned wary. "What about it?"

"You'll leave after this weekend, right? Do you think Romeo will be invited to work here while you're gone?"

Rian's eyes hardened. "Selena wouldn't have offered him the position if she assumed it was only while I was around. Believe me, until you, Mara, I hardly stayed in town. She understands that."

Mara stepped back to him, wrapping her arms around his waist, ignoring what it meant that he'd stayed longer because of her. "I'm sorry. I didn't mean anything by it." She rose on her toes and kissed his cheek.

"Selena is incredibly kind. If she can manage to live with my cranky brother, she can watch over a fourteen-year-old."

Giving in to the moment, she pressed her lips along his jaw, and then to his neck. "Why are you so dang tall?" she murmured as she trailed slow kisses down his throat, his five o'clock shadow scruffy on her lips.

"I can solve that." He brushed past her, grabbing her hand at the last second, tugging her to the sofa.

Were they just supposed to sit on the sofa and make-out like two teenagers with a restaurant full of people right outside the door? His brothers had to know why he'd brought her in there. That was embarrassing enough.

He sat down.

Mara moved to sit beside him. He gripped her hips, bringing her close enough that she had no choice but to straddle him or fall on top.

"Now I see why you locked the door." She liked the change in position. She was in charge. Cradling his face in her hands, she kissed him long and slow.

It wasn't an explosion. No. The burn from their kiss started in her toes and spread to her limbs like she'd just taken a shot of whiskey.

He pushed the kiss quicker, but she wouldn't budge the pace. The muscles along his shoulders tensed the longer she stayed in charge. Damn, she wanted to analyze it. Was it because he wanted more and was impatient? Did he ever take his time with a woman?

She didn't really want the answer to that last question.

His hands gripped her hips tight, and he broke the kiss. "This is killing me."

"Really?" She kissed him again. "I'm enjoying myself."

"It's torture."

She smiled.

He ran his hands up and down her back. "If torturing me makes you smile like that, I guess I'm in for some pain then. Kiss me, again before my brother's drag me back out there to figure out what to do about Philip."

She kissed him. Everything she had was put into that kiss. The heat between their bodies doubled. The slow torment from before had shifted into a raw intensity that made her wish their Saturday night was tonight.

His hands slipped underneath the edge of her shirt and over her skin along her back. "God, I want to touch you, Amara," he mumbled against her neck as he pressed his lips to her throat. "You know you can always change your mind, but for now, for my sanity, promise me I'll have you tomorrow night."

Backing out wasn't even in the playbook at this point. She nodded.

He lifted his head, his eyes a dark shade of blue. Darker than she'd seen them before. "I want the words."

She took a breath, the faint trace of the ocean from his cologne didn't help as she tried to steady her voice. "You'll have me Saturday."

Saying those words at his request, watching his lips part as he blew out a controlled breath, made her feel sexy. Hot. Alive.

Before she kissed him again and bumped up the date to *right* then, she stood up and stepped away. "I'm sorry I kept you from your brothers."

He half-laughed and adjusted his black T-shirt. "I don't care. They've imposed on me enough times." He kissed her on her forehead and moved toward the door. "But we need to leave so that I don't figure out how to speed up time so Saturday night can start right now. We won't ever make it to your parents' house." He held open the door and motioned her through. "After you."

She walked out, head held high. His brothers both stopped their conversation when she approached. "I hope y'all have a nice night."

Brogan rose and nodded. "You, too, Mara."

Cathal winked and toasted her with his beer. She smiled and walked out of O'Keeley's with the same swagger she had coming in.

13

"I had no idea you were seeing someone." Betty, Mara's childhood best friend, rubbed sunscreen over her pale, freckled skin, watching the five men in the front yard measure and cut the beams to replace the ones damaged in the hurricane. "Why is it over eighty in October?"

"It is hot," Mara mumbled as she glanced around. All the women were outside, watching the men. Her mom and aunt had their heads bent together, their hair colors an identical shade of gray. They rocked slowly in the porch chairs and gossiped about something, but a few times, Mara had caught them watching the men.

Even her annoying neighbor, Laura, made an appearance, her mouth moving a mile a minute having cornered Nessie, Mara's younger sister.

Rian actually looked like he knew what he was doing. It shouldn't surprise her. Each time he'd been faced with anything since she'd been around, he'd handled it with ease. Screwing beams together was no different.

"We aren't serious." Mara wished it was, but something

still held him back. She couldn't get into a committed relationship with a man who she didn't fully know.

"But you're dating him, right?" At Mara's silence, Betty set a hand on her hip. "Mara, no man is going to drive to Alabama for a long day with *your* family if he's not looking for something more than a tennis partner."

"I don't even know if he plays tennis."

She waved her hand in the air. "You missed the point. Have you noticed that he doesn't like Shane?"

Mara rolled her eyes. "How do you possibly know that? Rian has been pleasant to Shane. If anything, Shane has been an absolute jackass to Rian. He doesn't have any reason to like him."

"But he's your ex. I saw the way he reacted when Shane came in and kissed you like you were still a couple. Rian is definitely not a fan of another man touching you."

Mara had warned him about Shane again on the ride over. She knew he'd do something stupid like that. His smell, that overused cologne, clung to her afterward.

Laura made a giggling sound. Mara and Betty both looked up. Shane had taken his shirt off and tossed it to the side. The man was jacked. He spent more time in the gym than actually earning a paycheck. That was one of several reasons Mara left him and never looked back. Being used for money, regardless of how little she made, didn't appeal to her. Being told she needed to exercise or eat less, reminders she didn't have the perfect body, was another reason she'd walked away from Shane.

And then there was the yelling.

No one believed Shane had ever yelled at her when she'd told her mother that was one of the reasons they'd broken up. That hurt as much as Shane screaming at her that she needed to get her lazy ass up and workout. If he didn't get his way, he yelled. He'd never physically hurt her, but he'd scared the hell out of her more than a few times.

Rian caught her watching Shane. Guilt flooded through her. She hoped like hell Rian didn't think she had a thing for him. Mara snapped her head away.

Betty groaned. "Gross. Shane is doing that bouncy, pec thing he does. And Laura loves it. I swear those two are sleeping together. I didn't want to say anything before, but I wouldn't be surprised if they hadn't already slept together before you two broke-up."

"I was over that relationship long before we actually broke-up, so whatever." Mara didn't care about Shane and Laura. Shane could leave her parents' house and never return for all Mara cared. If Rian didn't already know that, he would as soon as she had a chance to tell him.

Betty cleared her throat. "Girl—"

Rian took long, easy steps across the dusty yard, reminding her of a dream sequence as he slowly lifted his shirt. Inch by inch, more and more fine chiseled skin appeared. Lean and toned.

The conversation on the porch ground to a halt. By the time the shirt was entirely off, he stood in front of the porch, looking up to Mara.

He held out his shirt. His eyes looked ocean blue in the sunlight and weren't subtle in their open attraction. "Can you hold this, Amara?" he asked in a quiet voice with his accent thick.

Mara reached down, took the shirt, and then swallowed. The man made her mouth water. He turned and walked back to the men. A tattoo across his back caught her eye. It looked like a thin snake made of words. But she couldn't make out what they said. His jeans rested low on his hips. None of the men paid him any attention except Shane.

"Staring is rude, Mara," her mom said, just loud enough for everyone on the porch to hear.

"No," Aunt Jemma chimed in. "Leaping off the porch and into his arms without asking for permission might be rude. Staring at that man is a privilege we should all thank the Lord and his mama for. I take back every negative thing I said about you dating a white guy."

"But you said you weren't dating." Laura shifted in the porch swing and rubbed her hands together. "Do you mind—"

"Yes." Mara ignored her aunt's loud cackle. "I mind." His shirt felt warm in her hands, and she resisted the urge to bring it to her face. It would smell like his cologne. His Irish skin wasn't tanned, but he wasn't pale, either. Just a warm, golden tone that she wanted to touch.

She'd get to touch.

She'd promised him tonight.

Betty sighed and set her chin in her hands. "Since we share everything, I'm completely ogling your man right now."

She almost corrected her but stopped herself. They had a family dinner later. A large family dinner that he didn't seem the least bit nervous to attend. But if a few of her female cousins had the least little idea that he wasn't her guy, it'd spell trouble. For her. And for him.

He probably had no idea what he'd just walked into.

Betty glanced over her shoulder at Mara. "Do you think he'd let me rub some sunscreen on him?"

Mara rolled her eyes.

"I need to go check the pork," her mom said as she rose gracefully from her chair. Her eyes locked onto Mara's. "You said he was going to cook something. Do you know what? How long it will take?"

"When you told us not to stop for groceries, that you had enough, he said he'd figure it out when he got here."

"Do you mind running out there and asking him? I'd hate to get in the way of a world-famous chef." The words were said with the nasty edge she'd probably intended, but her mom's lips twisted, and her eyes brightened. "I thought you were bringing home some pompous, old man when you called me and said your *friend* 'the chef' was coming with you."

"And now?"

Her mom's opinion shouldn't matter at this age. Not when it came to who she felt attracted to. Who she wanted to date. But it did.

"I'm glad my daughter and I share the same taste in men." She glanced over her shoulder. "He's very nice and respectful to you, which I appreciate." She held up her finger before Mara could get too excited. "But I don't care how many magazines he's been in or how much money he makes, as long as he doesn't mess up my kitchen or get in my way, I'll approve." She tilted her head to the side. "Go ask him what he wants to cook, baby."

She bounced off the steps, feeling lighter at her mom's tentative approval. She smiled as she approached Rian. Happy. It'd been a long time since she'd been home and felt happy. That was Shane's fault. Shane stood a few feet away, but with her eyes locked on Rian, she ignored his scowl.

Rian made her happy.

"God, you're beautiful when you smile that way." Rian's quiet praise brought her two brothers and dad to a sudden standstill. Shane crossed his arms and grunted.

Mara tucked her chin and looked at the ground. His feet appeared in her vision a brief second before his finger hooked underneath her chin, pulling it up. "Did you need something, *Agra*?"

"What did he call you?" Shane snapped out, throwing his shovel down. He snorted out his nostrils, like a crazed bull.

"Chill out," Bennett, her oldest brother said. Ever since he'd become a detective in Birmingham, he'd become the peacemaker in the family.

"Y'all don't even know this guy," Shane said, raising his voice. He pointed at Rian. "Just shows up out of nowhere, driving Mara's car. The man probably doesn't even have his own car. Just some lame ass cook in a restaurant expecting Mara to support him."

Rian's eyes narrowed a fraction. She'd never seen him mad or angry. It was one of the reasons she was attracted to him. Shane had an overload of testosterone. She definitely didn't want them to fight. Shane didn't mean anything to her and wasn't worth it.

"Knock it off, Shane," Mara said. She looked to her dad for help, but he raised one eyebrow. Great. No help there. He'd probably say it was too hot to worry about it.

Jaxon, her younger brother, wasn't any help either. He actually went back to measuring the wood. Humming. Bennett was the only one still watching the male staring contest between Rian and Shane.

"You can't be serious with him. I mean. Look at him," Shane said.

She crossed her arms, shifting to stand in front of Rian to face Shane. "I have looked at him. And talked to him. I don't know why you even care, Shane."

"Because you brought him here to make me jealous. Well, I'm not jealous of some pansy-ass cook."

"Shane—"

"No. You'll finally listen to me, Mara." Shane's jaw bunched. He took a step closer. He'd never fully shown his aggression in front of her family before. And even with her brothers, dad, and Rian standing there, that familiar fear zapped through her limbs.

The heat from Rian's body, so close behind her own, reassured her a little.

"He'll never understand you the way I do. You know I love you. I have since we were ten years old. We were supposed to get married." Shane grasped a hold of her shoulder. "I don't know why you won't see that."

He'd done nothing but tear her down. She just hadn't realized it until she moved out on her own, got out of the small town and realized how much she'd relied on him. How much he controlled her. Her feelings. Her thoughts.

"Let go of me," she demanded, shifting away. Or trying to. His grip wouldn't allow her to move.

He pulled her closer. "We need each other."

"I don't need you."

Rian's hands anchored her in place.

Shane lowered his voice and squeezed his hands around her upper arms. "Yes, you do. Look at you. All you've done since you left me is let yourself go."

"Let go of me," she said louder.

"She said, let go." Rian's voice was deeper, harder than she'd ever heard it.

"I'll let you go when I'm damn-well ready!" He shouted.

"Stop!" She stepped back, assuming she'd find Rian. But Rian stepped in front of her, his back blocking her view of Shane. Shane's hand released her.

"Dude—" Bennett moved toward her at the same time, shock registering on his face.

Taking one long, slow step at a time, Rian backed up

Shane.

Shane might have had muscles, lots of them, but good God, Rian seemed huge at that moment. And mad. Tall. Broad-shouldered. His finger, pointing in Shane's face. Growling something about "his Mara" while he dropped in and out of Irish. And maybe French. He didn't shout, but no one could question the fury in his words.

Bennett stepped between them. Mara expected Rian to go after Shane again. Instead, he turned and came to her, cupping her face in his hands as though she would break if he touched her.

"Are you alright?" He skimmed his thumb along her temple. "Don't shut down on me."

The breath she'd held rushed out. "I'm fine." Scared. Of Shane. And now, of Rian a little. She'd have never thought his easy-going, quiet personality, could switch that way.

But it was impossible to be scared with the way Rian held her, looked at her like she was the center of the universe. He'd dated exotic women all over the world, she'd seen the pictures on the Internet, and here he was, protecting her from Shane in her parents' front yard in her podunk hometown.

She set her hands on his shoulders. His skin under her fingertips, warm from the sun, anchored her. Not in reality. In reality, she had a rent payment she could barely make and ate frozen stir fry for dinner. But here, in this one moment, with him. His eyes. That light scent of aftershave that still clung to him. The way his chin dipped in just in the middle. She felt anchored.

She rose on her toes, kissing him lightly. Shane said something, but she couldn't process anything but the feel of Rian's lips against hers.

She tilted her head, wanting more from the kiss, not

caring about the audience. It happened every time they kissed. There were no sweet, simple kisses between them. Those were nothing more than a cover, a blanket holding in the heat that ran between their bodies.

His hands didn't move from their gentle grip on her face, but his body turned rigid. Did he not want this? She pulled away, but his hands kept her from retreating.

"Tonight," he murmured, his eyes searching hers.

She nodded.

He was right. They shouldn't start something they couldn't finish. Not the way both their bodies seemed to need the same thing. She couldn't kiss him the way she wanted to in the front yard with her family watching.

Because they were watching. Her brothers looked agitated at Shane.

Shane shot them one last furious glare before he stormed toward his car. Her dad, well, he seemed amused. He nodded his head once before rattling off orders for Bennett and Jaxon to keep working.

Mara stepped away, touching her hair and pretending she cared what it looked like. "Mom wanted to know what you planned to cook for supper. You told me you'd figure it out when you got here."

He glanced over his shoulder at her dad. "Do you mind if I go help your wife in the kitchen?"

Her dad set his hands and his hips and studied Rian. "You know, if any other man had asked me that, I'd have serious doubts about him seeing my daughter." He kicked his chin toward the house. "But please go find something I can eat that won't give me heartburn. I swear that woman is trying to send me to an early grave."

"I'll try, sir." He took his shirt off Mara's shoulder. She'd forgotten it was even there. "You can lead the way."

14

Mara's kiss in her parents' yard made their night together feel as though it'd never arrive. The sexy way her hands had tightened on his shoulders sent his mind to places it shouldn't travel with her da a few steps away, watching.

Judging.

Apparently, Rian had passed some unplanned test with her da.

Now, he needed to figure out her ma. It was strange, trying to navigate Mara's parents. The only other set of parents he'd met was back at nineteen when Sophie became his wife. But now he was in Mrs. Andrew's kitchen trying to impress the woman.

He stared into her refrigerator, trying to come up with something to make. It needed to win over her family, not win an award.

No pressure.

"What do you think?" Mara murmured beside him. She shifted closer, their bodies touching. Her shoulder, breast, hip all pressed against his side as she looked in the refrigerator. Every lush curve he wanted to feel was right there, off-limits with her ma standing five feet behind them.

He forced his hands to relax. He'd get the chance to touch her later.

"What about those potato things you made for the kids?"

He shot her a sidelong glance. "No." Her eyes had small flecks of gold in them. Had he noticed that before?

"She has the ingredients to make potato salad?" Her tongue darted out, wetting her bottom lip.

He gripped the door tight again. "No."

She reached across him, so close that he'd have to barely move to press his lips along the curve of her neck. "Look, here's some cabbage. You can make coleslaw."

He sighed and pinched the bridge of his nose. "No, Mara." Her proximity made it hard to concentrate. Her ma expected him to make something to serve the forty guests coming later, and all he could think about was Mara.

Mara crossed her arms and grumbled, "I can go back outside if you want to be alone."

She must think he was bothered by her. And he was. But not to have more distance between them. Maybe if he had a second with her, it'd take the edge off. That episode with Shane left him shaken. Not for the confrontation. He never fought like his brothers did, but he wouldn't back away.

But the *want* to fight caught him unaware.

No. Not fight. Protect.

He lowered his voice. "Can we talk somewhere?"

Her forehead produced a deep "V," and she mumbled, "yes." She turned and almost stormed out of the room. He ignored Mrs. Andrews' raised eyebrows.

Mara walked down the hall and turned into what appeared to be her brother's room.

He pushed the door closed.

Mara crossed her arms. "Did you want to talk?"

He crooked his finger and motioned her toward him. "Not especially. You make it impossible to concentrate on coleslaw and potato salad." When she took a hesitant step, he snagged her front belt loop and tugged her the rest of the way. With his back against the door, making damn sure no one could barge in, he hauled her to her toes and kissed her.

This shouldn't be this intense. The attraction to her body. Her laugh. Her smile. The way she huffed when she got annoyed. She wouldn't doubt his desire once he got her back to his condo. Although, for the moment, making out in secret like teenagers worked wonders to clear his head.

Her soft hands slid underneath his shirt, greedy. She touched him with a hunger that only brought his own starvation to his mind.

"God, I want to touch you," he whispered against her ear before trailing kisses along her neck. She smelled like the peach hand cream she kept in her car. The one she'd used on the way to Alabama that made the ride a little more than uncomfortable.

Her hands stilled along his back. He hated those sudden, small shifts where she went from being the woman he knew to worried. Scared. Of what? Who?

Shane? He'd seen the way she froze while Shane got louder and louder. It was all he could do not to knock that idiot into the next county.

"What's wrong?" He leaned away far enough to see her face.

She shook her head.

"I would never do anything you didn't want me to do. You know that, right?"

Her eyes widened. "It's not that. I just—I'm not very good at this."

"At what?"

"Being physical with someone. I'm a little worried about tonight."

Shane had damaged her confidence. He may not make the rounds like his brother Cathal, but he'd been with enough women to know how fragile their egos were. The same as men. One wrong word or action took a thousand good ones to make up for it.

"Amara." He said her name softly, enjoying the sound of it in his accent. He took her hands, placed them back on his chest. "Every time you touch me, I unravel a little more." He skimmed his hand along the curve of her waist, resting it at the top of her hip. "Every time I touch you, I have to tell myself to hold back."

"You don't have to," she whispered. She watched him with more trust than he deserved. She was made to settle down, start a family. At some point, he'd have to tell her he couldn't have children. For the time being, he'd committed himself to her the best way he knew how. He wouldn't look or touch another woman while with Mara. She deserved that respect. That didn't mean he could give her more.

"I'm not sure your brother would appreciate me tossing you on his bed at this moment."

She smiled. "No. I'm sure Jaxon wouldn't like the thought of me naked in his bed."

Rian let out a long, controlled breath. "I *really* like the thought of you naked in my bed."

"Tonight."

"And you haven't changed your mind?"

She initiated another kiss. He let her set the pace like she'd done the night before. For the next few weeks, he would be in her life, he'd let her take the lead when it came to the physical side of the relationship. It would keep her from having regrets later. That would kill him more than anything else.

A knock at the door made her jump away. "Y'all two come on," Betty's voice whispered.

Mara opened the door.

Betty grinned at Rian. "You better get in there and help Mrs. Andrews cook before she suspects more than she does."

Mara crossed her arms. "I'm pretty sure Mama knows I've kissed a boy before."

"Yeah, but not one that is here to try and show her up in her own kitchen."

"I'd never do that." He'd never want even to imply that to a hostess.

"That's what I heard her tell Nessie."

Rian placed a kiss on Mara's temple before walking away from both of the women. He knew how to win Mrs. Andrews over. At least he hoped he did. The afternoon would provide exactly what he needed at that moment. Education and a distraction.

Because in another few seconds, he would have written Jaxon an apology letter about his bed.

He walked into the kitchen and right to the sink, washing his hands. "You know, Mrs. Andrews, instead of cooking any of my recipes, I think I'd rather just help you."

"Help me?" She raised her eyebrows. "What? You don't think we'd enjoy your fancy food here?"

"I'd rather have the opportunity to learn how you cook your dishes. I've traveled extensively, always looking for a new way to fuse my culture with others. I've not had the opportunity to watch someone actually make Southern comfort food from scratch before." He grinned the way his sister-in-law, Selena, always teased him for doing. It was his version of puppy dog eyes. But a little more adult. "Please."

Mrs. Andrews studied him. "I'm trying to see if you're playing me."

"No, ma'am. Amara has raved about your food, and I'd love a chance to see how it's prepared."

A small, barely visible dimple appeared next to her lips. "Then grab that cabbage from the table and the food processor. You're about to make coleslaw."

He probably knew eleven different ways to make coleslaw, so he let her direct him.

The same with cornbread. He held the cast iron frying pan in his hand, loving the heavy feel. Each culture used different types of pots and pans and utensils. Discovering them never grew old. He'd worked with cast iron before, though. It might be something to keep in mind for the competition against Philip.

"I hope you're well introduced now," she teased after he'd held the pan a few moments. "Put some of that grease in there and put it in the oven to heat. We'll pour the cornbread batter in there with the hot oil. Gives it a nice crust."

By the time they worked their way through the meal, he was hot, tired, and having a good time. Mrs. Andrews also boasted a big smile as she introduced him to Amara's family.

"Does it feel weird?" Mara asked as she sat down beside him to eat at the long table. Twelve of Mara's family squeezed around the dining room table, some more at the card table in the corner, and the rest at picnic tables outside in the yard.

"Does what feel weird?"

"Being the only white guy in the room?"

He scanned the room. "No. I travel all over the world. I'm frequently the only white guy in a group. Not to mention the only Irishman. I'm loosely Catholic as well." He leaned closer, brushing his lips along the edge of her ear and whispering, "It's going to be painful to sit beside you through dinner."

Her hand touched his thigh briefly before drawing away. "You better stop. My mom has eyes like a hawk."

A quick glance at her mother, seated four people away at the long table, confirmed her eyes pinned on the two of them. But she smiled at Rian.

"I think your ma likes me."

Mara twisted her lips to the side and reached for her water glass.

He nudged her. "What?"

"I don't think she likes you for the same reasons I do."

"Don't tease me." He shifted even closer. God, in another moment, he'd drag the woman into his lap. Or revisit Jaxon's bedroom. "Why do you like me?"

"You really want to know?" She shifted, putting a barricade between her and the person seated beside her. "I feel like I'm feeding your ego."

"My ego isn't nearly as full as you think it is. I'm curious. I mean, looking at us, we don't appear to have anything in common."

She interlaced her fingers with his, out of sight of the rest of the dinner party. "No. I don't guess on the surface we do. I wouldn't say opposites attract, but I think we complement each other." She focused on their hands. "You make me laugh. And smile. You're close with your family, and I'm close to mine. Before you, my life went from frozen meal to frozen meal."

"So, you like me for my cooking?"

"This probably doesn't make sense, but, until you, it felt almost like I was stuck. Not just a daily routine. But in my mind. I realize that we aren't headed down the aisle, but my life is moving forward again because of you. My career. Emotionally."

He knew the feeling too well. He kissed her knuckles, ignoring the curious glances at their semi-private conversation.

"You're an amazing woman."

She leaned close, bringing their lips in line but not kissing him. "Of course, you're kinda cute, too."

"You're kinda cute yourself."

"I'm looking forward to tonight."

He set his hand on her knee, needing to touch her. "It's going to be the longest damn drive back to Atlanta—"

"Don't you two look cozy." Shane's voice brought Rian to his feet. Not the words, but the tone. Threatening. He recognized it easily.

Shane stood in the doorway, arms crossed with his bulky muscles stretching his T-shirt. "I'm not a fan of you touching my woman."

Rian shifted, standing in front of Mara. He wouldn't fight Shane. The rush to protect her from the asshole overpowered his rational thought to stay seated and look unaffected, though.

A brawling chef would make the papers, but for the wrong reason.

Mara's father sat at the table, still eating, ignoring the outburst. Bennett took a step but remained a few seats away.

"Shane, don't start something." Mrs. Andrews walked from her end of the table to stand beside Rian. "Mara made it clear she wasn't interested in being with you. By the way you're acting, I can't say that I blame her. You're welcome to join us for dinner, or you can leave."

"I'm not sitting at the table with him." Shane glared at Rian. "He's just some damn cook."

Mrs. Andrews took a step in front of Rian. It was hard not to pull her back and away from Shane, but she held up her finger. "You will *not* use that language at my table. You can sit down and eat and be civil or leave. But, I *swear*, you open your mouth, and those foul words come out again, this will be the *last* time you step foot in my house."

Right then, Rian knew Mrs. Andrews and his ma would have gotten along.

Shane puffed out his chest one more time and then left, slamming the door on his way out.

Mrs. Andrews turned and looked up at Rian. Her voice shifted from stern to sweet. "Rian, would you like some more coleslaw?"

15

Mara felt herself lift into the air. She jerked awake, her hand slapping Rian's shoulder. "Sorry!"

"I'd hoped not to wake you." He carried her from the car and to his condo building, past the doorman holding the door open. She must have fallen asleep on the ride home from Alabama.

And now he carried her like a child. Oh no. That wouldn't work. Not with where their night was headed.

"You can put me down."

He adjusted his grip, the hand under her thigh squeezing a little tighter. "I think I like you right here."

She wasn't a lightweight, a fact that made her want to demand he put her on her feet. "Please."

He set her down once they stood in front of the elevators. His hand didn't leave her lower back, guiding her onto the elevator once the doors opened.

"Sorry I fell asleep."

"I'm glad you got some rest." He leaned against the wall, arms crossed, looking entirely at ease.

She'd meant to talk to him about Shane on the ride

home, apologize for the scene he caused at dinner. Right then, Shane was the last person on her mind.

They stood watching one another, his heated gaze reminding her of a cat when it's about to pounce. His eyes were nearly amber in the soft glow of the elevator lights. The sound of late-nineties soft rock didn't fit their situation or her thoughts at all.

The elevator chimed, signaling his floor. "After you," he said and swept his arm out.

"I don't remember which apartment is yours." Lie. She stepped to the side, and he passed her, his expression thoughtful. Odd, since she assumed that he would throw all his charm her direction.

He unlocked his door and motioned her inside. "Here we are." At her hesitation, he pressed a hand along her lower back. "It's clean. I'm the cleanest one of the family."

His apartment hit her the same way as last time.

Mostly empty. Stark. Black and white. Devoid of color or feelings. She pressed a hand to her stomach. Something was off. The man just carried her into the building, watched her with enough heat to make her clothes smoke, and then his condo felt like an emotional icebox.

She half laughed. God help him if he ever had to venture to her apartment. Organized chaos.

"Mara?"

She turned to face him. His lips twisted into a small, sly smile. "You didn't listen to anything I just said, did you?"

"'Fraid not."

He held out a glass of wine. "Here. I was saying that your mom's cooking really inspired me. I'm not sure what I'm going to do with it yet, but I need to experiment."

"Just try adding a little butter or bacon. My mom always told me that. Not that her advice helped since I don't cook.

Neither butter nor bacon goes well with frozen orange chicken with rice."

His eyes narrowed. "Your meals sound horrible."

She lifted a shoulder, taking a sip of her wine. "It's easy and quick."

"Not everything easy and quick is better." He took a slow step closer to her. She could still smell his cologne, although faint. But with that familiar smell, he also smelled warm like the sun from being outdoors.

"Are we still talking about food?"

"No." He touched the outside of her hip.

She shifted, unaware she'd done so until his eyes narrowed. "Don't back away from me again." He brushed a curl away from her face. "Unless I'm doing something wrong."

She tried not to purr as he stroked his finger along the line of her neck.

"I'd like you to stay with me tonight, Amara." He took her wine glass from her and set it on the counter, never releasing her hip. "You gave me a taste of you today at your parents' house. I want more. I want as much as you're willing to give me."

Her breath quickened as his body came closer, her focus on his lips. After he held onto her other hip, locking her in place, she finally lifted her gaze to his. "What if all I want to give you is a kiss?"

"I'd say I'd take it and be a happy man." Their bodies pressed against each other, his hands sliding from her hips to her waist. "And try my hardest to convince you to give me more." From her waist to her ribcage.

Apparently, the same man that was into fine wine and exotic food enjoyed torturing her as well.

His thumbs brushed the underneath side of her breast. Her breath caught.

She either needed to swim or get out of the damn pool.

Starting at his wrist, she gradually ran her hands up his arms and rested them on his shoulders. "Do you think you're that persuasive?"

His hands gripped the bottom of her shirt, tugging it down. He took a deep breath. "I'd like to try."

Slowly, as if in a fog, she raised her arms.

He lifted her shirt up and over her head.

She didn't resist. One word and he'd have backed off. But she wanted this no matter what happened tomorrow. She regretted walking away from him each time. She was done living with regrets.

Her first instinct was to cover up. The lights were on.

But she forced herself to relax. His eyes took her in, scanning down her body. She waited for him to point out some flaw, an imperfection that a few extra hours at the gym might solve.

"Good God, Mara," he mumbled, his hands gliding along her waist and leaving a warm tingle in their wake. "I feel like I should promise to give you the best night of your life, but I feel horribly selfish, seeing as having you in my bed will be the best night of *my* life."

"You don't have to say that." He'd had models. Actresses. Socialites. She'd seen the pictures in the gossip magazines.

"It's the truth." He held her chin between his fingers, tilting her head up until she met his gaze. "I won't insult your intelligence and deny that I've been with other women, but, I promise, none of them compare to the woman I have standing in front of me."

She opened her mouth, but he pressed his finger over her lips.

"Don't argue with me." He kissed her, a quick touch of his lips to hers. "Just let me show you."

She wanted, needed to believe him no matter how ridiculous it sounded. She'd seen those women in magazines. Her brain tried to list out the reasons that she didn't measure up, but all thoughts came to a halt when Rian took his shirt off.

Those models he'd dated probably have some sexy line they'd feed him. Something sophisticated. Alluring.

Mara could barely contain the giggle when she finally got to touch the body that she'd watched all afternoon.

"I figured you might like things fair between us." He grinned, playful, and sexy.

She pushed her insecurities away and kicked them out of her mind for the night. She'd live in her own fantasy world and enjoy herself.

She allowed herself to smile the way she felt inside and not hold back. Her hands ran over his chest and across his abs. "Where's your bedroom?"

"This way." He snapped out the words before leading her across the barren living room.

Rian turned on the bedroom light. The room was just as sparse. A large bed with a dark bedspread and white walls. No pictures.

Across his back was the tattoo she'd seen earlier at her parents' house. Her finger traced the words as she spoke them.

"*To the waters and the wild, with a faery, hand in hand.*"

Rian's body stiffened.

"Who wrote that?"

"Yeats," he mumbled before looking down at his hands. The pain in his voice broke her heart.

She set her hand over the words, in the center of his

back, trying to comfort him. "Do you want to tell me what that means?"

"Not tonight." He turned. "I can't tonight." Wherever his mind had traveled had put a soulful look in his eyes. He looked like he might shatter if she pushed. So she backed off.

For now.

She turned and flipped the light off.

He turned it back on. "I want to see you, Mara."

"I'm not ready for that."

He cupped her cheeks. "He can't hurt you. Not again. Would it help to talk about it?"

Reliving her relationship with Shane was not the foreplay she wanted. She held onto his wrists, tugging them gently away from her face.

She angled her head to the side, watching his expression. "Neither one of us wants to talk about the past. We're here, together." When he didn't make a move, Mara pressed her lips against the center of his chest. And again.

Finally, his body relaxed a little, and his hands began to move, along her back, down her hips.

He kissed her. Hard. Fierce. All the emotions seemed to pour into the kiss. She'd take it. Be there for him. Because she'd lied to him earlier. She didn't just like him. A part of her loved Rian O'Keeley. She'd give him what he needed and if he'd let her, try to help him heal.

She opened the top button of his jeans. She'd never been the dominant one in a relationship, either in or out of the bedroom. She'd only slept with Shane, doing what he liked. What he wanted. That version of Mara was gone.

Rian kissed her cheek, her neck, behind her ear. He unbuttoned and unzipped her jeans, pushing them down her hips.

The moment she stepped out of them, Rian backed her up against his bed until she didn't have a choice but to sit down. Taking advantage of her position, she tugged his jeans down a fraction. "You said things should be fair between us."

He grinned, a crooked smile that she loved. "You're right." He discarded his jeans.

She moved toward the headboard.

He followed, reaching out and snagging her ankle. He tugged her back down the bed. She laughed.

"I don't like you to run away from me."

At least the storm she'd seen in his eyes had disappeared. "I'm not running, I'm just trying to get on the bed."

He leaned over her, planting a hand on either side of her head. "Are you sure about this, Mara? You can always back out." His gaze ran down her body. "But I pray you don't. I've never begged a woman before, but I'm not above it with you."

"Do many women back out once you have them in your bed in their underwear?" She smirked, hoping to appear confident.

Rian shifted his bodyweight. His fingers brushed across her cheek with more tenderness than she'd expected. "Darling, Mara, you aren't just any woman to me."

The words hit her heart. For the first time, she would sleep with a man that made her feel treasured. Rian would leave again, traveling the world. This was only a small moment in his life, even though it meant everything to her.

She arched her back, unclipped her bra, and tossed it to the side. "No. I'm not going to tell you to stop."

His breath rushed out. "Mara." He paused a long

moment before touching her. She'd been scared that every aspect of sex would remind her of Shane.

Nothing. Not the way Rian's kisses trailed across her collarbone to her breast. Not the natural way the rest of their clothes disappeared. Definitely not the way Rian managed to make every inch of her body burn for him.

He touched, kissed, and lived up to his promise for her to have the best night of her life. He mumbled things in French about her being beautiful, sexy, before switching languages. For once, she believed it.

She then decided no longer to live with past shadows; she pushed him onto his back and crawled on top of him.

The man looked so hopeful at the change in position, it shamed her to lump him in the same category as her ex. Rian seemed to love her body. She should love her body, as well.

With the bedroom lights on, she ditched the last of her insecurities, sat up, and enjoyed herself.

16

Rian ran a finger along the ridge of Mara's spine as she laid partway across his chest. Last night changed him. Unexpectedly. He hadn't lied to her. None of the women in his past compared to Mara. That had been the truth.

He'd never gone deeper than mutual interests and common likes with the women he'd dated in the past. Type of food or wine. Art or movies. Current events. He'd never had a desire to find out more.

And then something about Mara made it necessary for him to learn everything about her. Having her in his bed could prove to be a significant distraction from what needed his focus at the moment. The competition.

"Do you ever invite your parents to Atlanta?"

Mara lifted her head. "If you're worried about them catching me sleeping with you, I'm fairly certain they figured it would happen eventually."

He loved her soft skin. As much as staying in bed all day sounded perfect, he needed to refocus on the competition and figure out a new dish. "No. It's not that. It was what you said last night."

Her eyes narrowed. "I don't think I want anything repeated in the light of day."

Laughing, he rolled over until she was underneath him. "Not that. Although you were quite unique." He nipped at her bottom lip. "When I mentioned trying to experiment with your ma's food. You said that she always told you…"

"Life is short—" she leaned up and kissed his neck "—lick the bowl?"

"Mara—"

She plopped back down. "Fine. Last night." Her forehead wrinkled a split second before clearing. "Try adding more butter or bacon?"

"Yes. That was it." He climbed off the bed.

"Hey!" She scrambled for the sheet to cover herself. "What happened to that sweet, morning after love-making I read about in romance novels?"

He grinned over his shoulder as he grabbed a pair of jeans from his dresser. "Mara, darling, I expect to persuade you back into my bed tonight. And tomorrow." The rest of the week if he didn't leave on Tuesday. "Right now, I need to call your mother and get started."

"No! Do not call her!" She snatched at her shirt on the floor beside the bed, tugging it on. "Especially not on Sunday. That woman will put me in the prayer requests at church."

Rian leaned against the door to his closet, her jeans were on the floor at his feet.

She narrowed her eyes. "You're not going to bring me my pants, are you?"

"Nope."

With a huff and a small smile, she tiptoed to her pants,

giving Rian the view he wanted. "Now, I definitely will be begging you to stay with me again."

With her clothes on, she could concentrate. "Why are you calling my mom?"

"To ask her to come to Atlanta and help me." He slipped his black T-shirt over his head. "I don't just want to beat Philip. I want to produce something amazing. I need to find that flavor I've been searching for over the past few years. The closest I've come to it was when I cooked with your ma. I thought of a dozen different ways to infuse our cultures on the drive back from Alabama."

Both the Irish and the South produced amazing comfort foods. He'd considered doing a high-concept dish, something deconstructed that had meaning behind it. For all he knew, Philip would try that. He wanted something that satisfied the soul.

"And you need my mother here to do it? Can't you just search on the internet for something?"

"You're joking?"

She winced. "Apparently."

"Your mom is an amazing cook. All I've done the past ten years is travel the world working with the best cooks."

"High-class chefs. Not women like us from Alabama."

He kissed her. God, why did she think so little of herself? "The best cooks I've worked with were in their homes. That's real food and real flavors. I grew up standing at an old stove in a home with one toilet and two bedrooms. That's one room for my brothers and me. I've cooked in five-star Michelin restaurants and at a small food stand on a corner in Seoul." He held out his hand for her. "Let me call her. Then I'll find us something quick to eat, and we'll go to your apartment for you to change."

Her face fell. "That's alright. You don't have to do that."

"Are you ashamed of me coming to your apartment?"

"I'm more fearful for your life. My cat is a little bit of a drama queen."

Rian waved her off and led her to the kitchen. "I've dealt with both Brogan and Cathal my whole life. A cat can't be much worse."

"She'll scratch you."

"So will Cathal if you wake him up while he's still scuttered. Now, give me your ma's number so I can give her a ring."

Mara sighed and rattled off the number as he typed it into his phone. "I still don't know why you need her to come here."

"Hello?" Mrs. Andrews answered on the second ring.

"Hello. This is Rian O'Keeley. Sorry to call so early on a Sunday, but I have a really important question to ask."

Mara closed her eyes.

Rian skimmed a finger along the curve of her cheek. God, she was gorgeous.

"I swear you and my daughter better not be planning on getting married this soon. That may work in Hollywood, with all those actresses and actors marrying each other right and left—"

"No." He jerked his hand away from Mara and shook his head just as hard. "No. No. Not at all. I wanted to invite you to Atlanta. I'm in a bit of a spot."

"Oh?" The relief in her voice from his declaration they were *not* getting married bothered him. "Is Mara alright?"

"Yes. She's just fine." He laughed lightly when the woman in question rolled her eyes.

"She's there with you, isn't she."

Rian froze. He hadn't anticipated broaching that subject. Mara mouthed, "What?"

He held up a finger and walked to the window of his condo, the view looking out over the skyline of Atlanta. A pretty view on Sunday morning even though Mrs. Andrews made him nervous as hell.

"Mara is old enough to make up her own mind. You just take care with her. She's not some model you run after. She has feelings and a heart. I don't want to see them get trampled on when you decide to move to the next woman."

Had she said it with a nasty edge to her voice, Rian might have had a witty comeback. As it was, said with such concern for Mara, he could only say, "I know," and nothing more. He'd take care of her heart because he cared for the woman. He wouldn't have invited her back to his bed, to his condo, had he thought of her as he did the other women he dated.

But digging into those feelings meant facing demons he wasn't ready to. Not yet.

"Good. Well. Have her call me later."

"I will. Wait! I didn't get to talk to you about why I called."

She chuckled. "You didn't call to discuss Mara?"

"No. I called to ask you about cooking."

"I appreciate the way you acted while you were here in my kitchen, but you and I both know that there's nothing I can do to help you with the type of food you cook. I know I gave you a hard time, but you are an amazing chef based on everything I've read."

"I told you when I was there that I was trying to come up with different flavors, trying to infuse where I live now with some of the Irish flavors from the countryside. I'm in a tight spot at the moment. A chef's version of writer's block."

Mara stepped beside him, resting her hand on his

forearm. He picked it up and kissed the back of her hand. Her support muddled his feelings even more.

"I'd like for you to come to Atlanta for a few days. I'll pay for a hotel. You can bring your husband or Nessie. Or no one if you'd like a holiday."

"What on earth do you think I can do once I'm there?" The excitement in her voice gave him hope.

"Work in the kitchen with me."

"In what kitchen?"

"My restaurant. Or my condo. Wherever we can find space, really. I'll explain more about the competition I'm in once you arrive, but this would be a big favor to me if you could help." He held his breath, waiting for an answer.

What would he do if she declined to help? He had a flight out Tuesday. He'd jet off to California and hope to find inspiration out there. And wish he was back in Atlanta with Mara and his family.

He'd never had those feelings of wanting to be home before.

Mara began to pace, looking at the ground.

"When did you want me to come?" Mrs. Andrews asked.

"Today, if possible."

Mara looked around the room, probably assessing his lack of personal touches again. She'd asked him last night about his condo. And his tattoo.

To the waters and the wild With a faery, hand in hand.

Impossible to think of the words and not feel that lump in his throat. No. He couldn't think about it now.

"I think we can come over after church today. And you need us to stay the night?"

"Yes. I'll put you up in a hotel near O'Keeley's. I'm scheduled to fly out Tuesday."

Mara stopped her pacing and looked at him, her expression shifting from contemplation to sadness.

Hell. He didn't want to leave.

The force of the thought made him turn away. Last night changed things.

"Rian?" Mrs. Andrews' voice brought him back to reality.

"Yes. Can you stay until Tuesday? I'll—" He glanced at Mara. "—I'll probably end up changing my flight plans with the competition anyway." He ran a hand over his head. Shit, he was in too deep already.

"I think we can manage that. It'll be nice to visit with Mara. We can stay with her. I don't want to cause you extra expenses at a hotel."

Rian put his phone on mute. "Do you want your parents to stay at your apartment with you and Dash, the cat?"

"Oh, God, no!"

He unmuted the phone, trying not to laugh as he answered. "You're going to help me, so I'd really appreciate being able to treat you and your husband."

Mara mouthed, "Thank you."

"Then, we'll head over to Atlanta after church today."

"I look forward to seeing you." He hung up.

"Why did you change your plans?" She crossed her arms. He hated her insecurity. He couldn't sort out his feelings at the moment and didn't have a clue what it meant that he'd rather stay in Atlanta with her than fly out to California. If she didn't have a career of her own, he'd beg her to go with him.

"I've not decided if I'm going yet. It took a little under three hours to make it to Atlanta from your house, right?"

Mara nodded.

Rian reached over his head and pulled his shirt off. "Then, if it's alright with you, I'd like to take you back to bed." He cared for her, but right then, he needed the distraction. He needed her.

"But what about breakfast?" She took a step backward, toward his room. "Weren't you hungry?"

He tossed his shirt to the sofa. "Absolutely." He unbuttoned his jeans and walked after her.

She laughed as he chased her into his room. He caught her around her waist, pulling her back against his body. His hands fisted in the bottom of her shirt. "I thought you liked to play fair?"

She shot a cute smile over her shoulder. "Always."

God, he was so screwed.

17

"Where's Daddy?" Mara held the door open for her mom to enter O'Keeley's. It was near dinnertime, and Rian had invited them both to the restaurant to eat before they'd go back to the hotel.

"Your daddy decided to stay in the hotel and check out the two hundred channels. He said he'd order something later." Her mom arched a manicured eyebrow. "Apparently, he doesn't care if Rian is footing the bill or not."

"Rian can afford it." She didn't have a clue how much he made, but based on his car and the condo, he wasn't hurting for money.

"You're not taking advantage of him, are you?" She raised the other eyebrow. "That's not why you're in this relationship?"

Mara ran a hand over her face. "No! Geez! I would never do that. You know me better than that."

"Okay, calm down. I just had to ask. You know he isn't exactly the type of man you date."

Mara nodded. "I get it. Because, you know, before him, I didn't date. Not really." Rian walked out of the office, his gaze sweeping the restaurant before settling on them. "But, I like him."

Her mom patted her shoulder. "I know, baby. Enjoy yourself. Your father is certainly enjoying himself on Rian's tab." She laughed and held out her hand to shake Rian's when he approached. "Hi."

"Glad you could make it, Mrs. Andrews."

"Call me, Lindsay."

He leaned down and kissed Mara on the cheek. "Is your father not here?"

Mara cut her eyes at her mom. "No. Long story. He's happy by himself at the hotel." She linked her arm through her mother's. "But we are here, and we are hungry."

"Good." He looked past her to the waitress. "Katie? Where do you want to seat us?"

A woman smiled brightly at Rian. "You're actually going to sit in the restaurant and eat your own food? I feel like I should take a picture and hang it on the wall."

Mara didn't know who Katie was to Rian, but she acted like a friend. A close friend. Mara tilted her head a little higher. Rian had been photographed with dozens of women over the years. Why did one cute waitress bother her so much?

Because his life in those magazines was far away. Here, in Atlanta, in O'Keeley's, it'd only been Rian and her. No other women to compete with. She sounded like a commercial for women with low self-esteem. Professionally, she was confident. She could run the center without breaking a sweat. But with Rian, she hoped the insecurity of wondering why he was with her would disappear. She couldn't go through a relationship, have a boyfriend or whatever he was, thinking she didn't belong with him.

Katie set the menus on the table. Rian held out Mara's

chair, and as soon as she sat down, Katie held out her hand. "I'm Katie. I'm Selena's best friend and soon to be Godmother of Rosie."

"Rosie? Rosie O'Keeley?" Rian sat beside Mara. "I hadn't heard Selena settled on a name."

"Oh, she hasn't. That's my vote. I like Rosie. You know, Rosie the Riveter." She made a muscle with a mean face.

Mara and her mother both laughed. She'd definitely judged Katie too quickly.

Rian shook his head. "I don't know what you're talking about. And Brogan might have muscles, but I'm not sure I want his daughter to look the same way."

Katie swatted at Rian and looked at Mara. "Will you please explain?"

Mara patted his shoulder. "Later."

"Thank you. I can't have Rosie's uncle not understanding her legacy. What can I get you to drink?" Katie asked.

"Sweet tea," her mom said as she scanned the menu. "What should I get to eat, Rian?"

Rian stared at the menu with disgust. "Nothing. It's all boring."

"You sound so snobby." Mara shook her head when he looked at her, shocked by the insult. "Seriously. You're so frustrated with trying to find something new to cook that you're taking it out on everything else you can cook." She took her mom's menu, hoping she wasn't pushing him and making his problem worse. But she'd listened to him complain when they finally crawled out of bed, and he cooked her breakfast. And then again, lunch. Everything he cooked was delicious, and he called it dull and tasteless.

"Go to the kitchen and cook Mom and me something new. Get out of your own head."

"Mara—"

"No." She glanced down at the menu, scanning it. "Mom likes fried fish. Do something with the fish and chips. Or don't fry the fish and do something else with it. Just go *create* something. That competition is in two weeks. You can't whine about it up until the night before, or else you'll definitely lose."

He pushed back from the table, looking unhappy. The worst he'd ever aimed those greenish eyes her direction. Katie stood to the side, her mouth hanging open.

He stalked away, shoving open the kitchen door with more force than necessary and disappearing inside before Katie moved again. "I've got to go tell Selena."

"What?"

Her mom *tsked* under her breath. "I raised such a bossy woman."

Mara held her hands up. "Listen, all day today he's been moaning about how everything he does is crap. Breakfast was amazing. Lunch was amazing." She pointed at Katie. "Please, go tell Selena. Maybe she'll have an idea. All I know to do is push him to make something." Because that's how she handled the kids. When they wanted to give up, she kept pushing and pushing until they broke through and it finally clicked. Rian might not be persuaded as easily as Blair with M&M's.

Katie nodded and moved toward the office.

"Breakfast, huh?" Her mom raised that one eyebrow again.

Shit.

She shook her head. "And you said you were just casual with that man? You treat him like a wife."

"I do not."

"Yes. You treat him like you believe in him. You know

what he's capable of and will push him to achieve it. That's being a supportive wife."

"We're dating. Don't mention anything serious or try to get too close." She crossed her arms and sat back. She still hadn't gotten him to explain his condo or the tattoo. "Not that I want to marry him or anything."

Her mom made a little humming noise as she squeezed the lemon into her tea. "Right, baby. I know."

"Believe me, if he acts like that with you in the kitchen tomorrow, I'm not sure what would be left of Rian's ear. You'll have chewed it off all day."

"Probably. But better he hears it from you than from me. I like him, Mara. More so that he's so driven for something in life." She clasped her hands together and leaned forward. "Your father never had any drive. And, until I saw you with Rian at my house, I never realized that I wanted you to have someone that matched you. Shane wasn't good for you. I see that now."

"What do you mean?" Her parents adored Shane.

"He was lazy. Rian is driven to be the best. You're the same way. Just wait, you'll see. With that man in your corner, you'll finally reach your potential. Because he'll push you the same way you pushed him." She nodded her head. "Now, tell me what's happening at the center lately. Are you any closer to getting the promotion?"

"Possibly. Not soon enough, I know that. My favorite kid, Romeo, got kicked out for fighting last week. He's coming here now."

"What do you mean?"

"He's coming to O'Keeley's after school. Rian said he'd watch him until Selena got the paperwork signed for him to work. It's a safe environment, and he needs the money anyway."

Her mom shook her head. "Isn't he around fourteen? That's too young to have a serious job, isn't it?"

"No. Not for Romeo. Rian and his brothers all swore they started working at that age. I think it will keep Romeo out of trouble until I can get him back into the center. Then, I thought we could see about him working a couple days and then coming to the center a few days." Because she did want to give Romeo a childhood. A break from thinking like an adult and surviving.

Her mom patted Mara's hand. "I'm so proud of the woman you've become, baby."

Mara swallowed, holding back the emotion of hearing the words. She'd felt so low for so long, it was hard to see her accomplishments. Even if she only made a difference in the life of one kid, it was enough.

Selena crossed the room, holding two plates. "Here. Sorry. Rian made these for you."

"It looks delicious." Her mom motioned to his empty seat. "Is he not eating?"

"Well—"

Mara sat back and looked at Selena. "What'd he say?"

"That you want him to be the chef, so he'll stay in the kitchen like the chef." She grimaced. "I tried to talk him out of that."

Mara pushed back from the table. "Please, mom, eat. I'll be back."

"Mara—"

She held her hand up, stopping her mom. "Don't let your fish get cold. Just give me a second."

THE DOOR to the kitchen swung shut as Selena left to take Mara and her mother their lunch. Mara had pushed him.

He'd hated it...but it'd worked. He'd been trying different recipes, techniques for the past few months. Forced to create something for the ma of the woman he was seeing, and make sure it was delicious, had helped.

But this was a unique situation. The crispy pan-fried cod wouldn't beat Philip. It wasn't unusual and outstanding. No amount of Mara's pushing would suddenly force the creativity that seemed to have disappeared back to the surface.

He hadn't had any useful ideas in months. And now, Philip had finally given him the conditions for the competition in an email he'd received a couple hours ago.

Philip wanted it at O'Keeley's.

And he wanted them both to pick the judges.

Both of those were fine with Rian. But he hadn't shared the prizes for the competition with his brothers. Philip wanted a personal endorsement of his restaurant. For a full year. Every magazine article, every interview, every time he mentioned O'Keeley's, Philip wanted Rian to mention Philip's restaurant as well.

And the idea of it made Rian's stomach turn over the same way it did when he smelled rancid meat. Saying anything nice about Philip's restaurant, after all the shit he put O'Keeley's through with the bad reviews, might drive him clinically insane.

But Rian used the stakes to his advantage.

Philip promised to make a donation to Mara's after-school center of twenty-five thousand dollars.

The door barely stopped swinging before Mara appeared. Her glare made him pause in patting out his burger.

"What the hell, Rian? You invite us to lunch and then ditch us?"

"I don't normally—"

She held up her finger. He'd imagined she'd done that to the kids at the center a few times in her life, but it was effective. He stopped talking.

"No. You don't get to act like some diva."

"Diva?" Odd word to use for him.

"Yes." She crossed her arms. "Right now, you're in here pouting because I pushed you to create something that I'm sure is absolutely delicious, and I'd like to go enjoy with my mom." She paused for a long second. "And my boyfriend."

The title should scare him, and it did, but it looked to make her more nervous, and that caused him to smile. "You consider me your boyfriend?"

She shrugged and glanced away. "That's the nicest thing I can think to call you at the moment."

He turned to the grill, set his burger on the hot surface, before motioning to the cook who handled that station to take over. Having a girlfriend meant she was his. At least for the time being. Rian walked to the sink and washed his hands. "Ah, Mara. I'll be your boyfriend if you'd like me to."

She huffed. "You're so cocky."

"Yes." He dried his hands. "Divas are usually cocky." He crossed the kitchen. She didn't budge from her spot. Her annoyance amused him, although he'd keep that to himself. "I didn't like you pushing me."

"Everything you have ever cooked for me has been delicious."

"I can do better."

The tension in her shoulders lessened, and her annoyance with him seemed to ease. "And that is why you'll win the competition. Give yourself time to work it out. You have two weeks, right? Get in the kitchen with Mom and see what you come up with. I can promise you, though, that she won't be any easier on you."

"I give her my permission to hit me with a wooden spoon, if necessary."

She lifted one shoulder and cut her eyes up at him. "I mean, I can do that if that's something you're into—"

He grinned. "I never knew that my sweet Mara had such a dirty mind."

She kissed him. "Come back to the table with us. Please."

"I will." He stopped her as she turned to leave. "Mara, you need to know that even without the title of boyfriend, if you're sleeping in my bed, no one else will be. In Atlanta or anywhere in the world. I hope you understand that."

"I'd hoped that was the case, but it is nice for you to confirm it." She reached out her hand, and he interlaced his fingers with hers. "Come on. My dinner's getting cold."

18

"Thank you for dinner, Rian." Mara's mom smiled, looking genuinely happy with Rian. Mara relaxed back. Dinner had been delicious, but it was a major victory to win Lindsay Andrew's approval. Not only her support but to cook her something and her not point out every flaw. Although, maybe she only did that with Mara's attempts in the kitchen. After Mara swore that boxed macaroni and cheese tasted the same as the real thing, her mother never recovered.

"You're welcome." Rian rested his arm along the back of Mara's chair, a foot crossed over his knee, looking relaxed. Confident. Charming.

His thumb skimmed along the back of her neck, concealed by her hair. She clasped her hands, focused on whatever her mom told about her sister, and not on the unspoken reminder of their time together.

After last night, she'd developed a heightened sense of awareness about him. The way he moved. The way he spoke. The little excuses he found to touch her. How did everything turn her on now?

Did all the women he dated have this strong of a reaction to him? It was like he was in those damn men's cologne commercials, the ones with the women tripping and stumbling over themselves to get at the guy. Only Rian didn't smell like a bottle of cologne.

All he had to do was cut his eyes in her direction, and she was hooked again.

"What are we cooking tomorrow?" her mom asked.

Rian sat forward, ending his torture, and set his hands on the table. "I'll have three things to try out, but I'm still deciding at this point."

Excitement crept into her mom's voice. "And are we cooking here or at your apartment?"

"Let's cook at my apartment. I don't want other people getting in the way." Rian leaned toward Mara, his hand landed on her thigh underneath the table. *High* up on her thigh. His eyes held every suggestive thought darting through his mind. "You have work tomorrow, right?"

"Yes." The word left her mouth with a squeak.

The man grinned, his hand tightening before disappearing. "Too bad."

She shook her head. "It will be better with just you and my mom cooking. I think I can safely say you are the two best cooks I know."

"Can you convince Mara to cook instead of eating those frozen dinners?" her mom asked.

Damn. Would no one leave her frozen beef fried rice alone?

"I offered to make her frozen dinners myself."

Her mom's eyes widened. "That's very generous of you. I hope she takes you up on your offer."

"We could even cook them in her apartment." He picked

up her hand, bringing it slowly to his lips. "If she'd invite me over." He kissed her skin and winked.

Last night, she felt sexy and in charge.

Today, with her mom sitting across from her, she sat there dumbfounded. Suffocated by her own desire.

"Excuse me," she mumbled. Jumping up from the table, she walked to the bathroom in the back corner of the restaurant.

She paced the empty room, thankful for the air conditioning as she tried to get a handle on the situation. Her response was unnatural. No one should want to crawl all over their boyfriend's lap while sitting across the table from their mother. But he did that to her.

She could control herself.

She stopped, took another deep breath, and opened the bathroom door.

Rian stood there, arms crossed, that amused expression on his face. "Are you alright?"

"Do you always follow your dates to the bathroom?" She started to brush past him.

His hand wrapped around her upper arms and tugged her into a room on the opposite wall. He closed the door. And locked it.

A light flicked on a moment later. The supply closet.

"You're driving me crazy, Amara."

Her mouth dropped open. She pointed at herself. "Me? Me? I'm not the one touching and stroking and kissing hands. I had to get away from you before I embarrassed myself in front of my mother. Who, by the way, is like freaking Sherlock Holmes and will definitely put two-and-two together if we're both gone from the table."

He crooked his finger. "I'm not worried about your mother. Come here."

She crossed her arms, trying to look stern, but a smile broke through. "No."

"Mara." He took a slow, predatory step in her direction. The whole situation amused him. "I want a kiss, and then we'll go back to the table."

"Rian—" She held up her hands a second before he snatched his arms around her waist and pulled her to him.

She laughed as she playfully struggled to escape. Twisting in his arms, she gripped his shoulders. "Fine. One kiss and then stop all the touching. I'm serious."

"If you say so." He lowered his head, brushing his lips over hers. "Is that your one kiss?"

"Shut up," Mara muttered and then tugged him down for the kiss she wanted.

One kiss wasn't enough. It would never be enough. Not the way Rian kissed. It reminded her of the way he cooked. Beautiful. Elegant. And somehow, she didn't feel like a total clod trying to keep up with him.

He moved his hand along her thigh, over her hip, under her shirt, and rested over her bra.

"Is that your one kiss?" he asked, his fingertips brushing the silky skin along the edge of her bra.

"You're driving me crazy."

He smirked, and his fingers still tormenting her. "I don't see how that's bad."

Mara rested on hand on his belt buckle. "Do I need to reciprocate the torture?"

Rian's eyes narrowed, and he glanced around. "Not here. No. My brother would probably kick me out of the family if he knew I was in here with you anyway." He stepped away. "Tonight. Come stay with me again."

"I'll let you know later. No telling what my mother will

say when we get back to the table. You may go running for the hills."

Rian set his arm over Mara's shoulders, unlocking the supply door and walking out with her. No shame. No worry that people will talk. He didn't seem to give a damn.

Why did she love it?

He held out Mara's chair, neither one of them giving any explanation to her mom. Her mom sat there, playing a game on her phone, as though they'd never left the table.

"I trust everything is alright?" her mom asked, her eyes flicking up to meet Mara's. Was her mom laughing at her?

Cathal cut across the restaurant to their table, his expression serious.

She tapped Rian on the leg. "Rian?"

Rian sat up a little straighter.

"Good evening," Cathal said as he stopped. He held out his hand to her mom. "I'm Cathal O'Keeley, Rian's brother. Do you mind if I borrow your daughter for a moment? I need her in the office."

"Me?"

Her mom raised her eyebrow, a signature look that Mara had tried to perfect with the kids at the center. "I don't suppose I do. She's already visited the supply closet."

Both Mara and Rian's mouths fell open.

"You were right," Rian said, complete awe in his voice.

"Just keep saying that, and we'll be alright." She brushed her hand along Rian's shoulder and followed Cathal back to the office. "Unless it's a disgruntled child, I'm not much use."

"No child yet." He closed the office door after she entered. The sound of someone getting sick was the first noise she heard.

"Oh. Selena?"

He crossed his arms and began to pace. "Yes. Brogan is gone for the moment, and I'm at a loss. I'd grab Katie, but she's working the floor, and we're already short-staffed because Selena was taking someone's shift tonight. I thought maybe you could help her."

"I'm not sure she'd want me in there. Did you get her any water?"

"Yes. That's about all I'm good for." He ran a hand through his hair. "The night that Brogan leaves me in charge of everything. I could probably screw up the restaurant, and he wouldn't care, but he's fiercely protective of Selena. I hate it that I can't help her."

Mara smiled. Poor Cathal. She patted him on the shoulder. "There's nothing you can really do. It's perfectly natural at this point in her pregnancy, but go ask Katie to come here. I'll take her tables. You go pick up Selena's shift, or else go behind the bar and kick the bartender to the floor."

"That's what Brogan would've probably told me to do, but you're a touch nicer in saying it." The sound of Selena getting sick again sent Cathal running out the door.

A moment later, Katie came in. "I'm here for Selena duty."

"Good. I know if I were in her position, I wouldn't want an almost stranger in there with me." She took the pad and pen from Katie. "I'm much better at waiting tables."

She left Katie to nurse Selena. Cathal stood behind the bar and looked less stressed while chatting with an older man who sat at the end.

Crossing the room, she stopped by her mom's table. "Selena has morning sickness."

Rian shook his head. "Are you sure it's not a virus? It's not morning."

Mara's mom set her napkin on her plate. "Morning sickness can happen at any time of day. When you have kids, you'll realize that."

A shadow passed over Rian's pleasant expression, his voice turning hard. "Who's with Selena now?"

"Katie. I'm going to take her tables." She leaned down and kissed her mom on the cheek. "I'll give you a call tomorrow."

Rian stood. "I'll take your ma to the hotel." The baby comment had changed his demeanor. They'd never talked about kids. They weren't at a point in the relationship where it would come up. It should be obvious, though, that she'd want children one day. And Rian was so good with Blair and Romeo.

She wouldn't ask him. Right now, she was happy he was committed to her. They still had to go through several more steps in their relationship before kids were a topic of conversation.

Mara worked the rest of the evening, waiting tables and laughing at whatever jokes she overheard Cathal tell at the bar. By ten, she was dead on her feet. Had waiting tables been this hard before? All she remembered were the fun times in high school and college. Amazing tips and sneaking food when the boss wasn't looking.

She went to the office to say goodbye. Selena sat alone on the sofa with a cup of tea. "Come in." She waved Mara forward. "I cannot begin to tell you how grateful I am for your help tonight."

"No problem." Mara sat down in the leather chair across from her. "How are you feeling?"

Selena set a hand on her stomach. "I'm not sure how I didn't throw up the baby at this point. Everything tastes so damn good and then *bam*, it comes right back up."

"When will Brogan be back?"

"I made his brothers promise not to tell him and sent him home after his meeting. He's been up every night with me, and it's starting to make him cranky. Cathal and Rian usually tell Brogan everything when it comes to me, but even they've taken the brunt of his sleeplessness and agreed to keep it between us for the time being." She sipped her tea and closed her eyes. "I want kids, don't get me wrong, but sometimes I wished I could have like a weekend pass to feel like myself again." She studied her teacup. "Do you want kids, Mara?"

"Yes. I love children." One of the reasons she'd chosen the job she did. "I'd like to be married first, though."

Selena nodded slowly. "How serious are you and Rian?"

That was an odd change of topic. "About having kids?"

"No." She set the cup on the table and folded her hands over her stomach. "No. Just in general."

"We're exclusive if that's what you mean."

Cathal walked into the office, his eyes locked on Selena. "How are you?"

"Better. The tea helped." She smiled. "Throwing up my brains for the past hour helped, too."

He set a hand on Mara's shoulder. "We appreciate your help, Mara. You saved the day."

"Not really." She stood up from the chair. "But I do need to go. I have an early morning with work." She rolled her ankles. "I'm suddenly glad I'll be sitting at a desk tomorrow."

Selena laughed. "I feel like that every time I have to work a shift, now. Goodnight, Mara."

The restaurant was empty as they passed through it. Most of the lights were already off. Strange, but it felt natural being a part of their small group. She liked them.

Selena. Cathal. Brogan. They all loved each other, which was easy to see.

And it was just as easy to forget that she was a temporary addition. Rian might be exclusive, but she still had a sinking feeling that he'd walk away at some point.

Cathal walked with her to the front of the restaurant. She assumed he'd stop there, but he followed her out the door.

"You don't have to escort me to my car. I'll be fine."

"No. Even without Rian's twenty phone calls asking how you were doing and making sure I saw you home safely, I'd walk you to your car." He slipped his hands in his pockets and glanced up at the sky. "You know, back home, the sky is filled with thousands of more stars than you can see in Atlanta. I don't miss much about leaving, but that's one of them."

Mara looked up. "I'd like to see that."

"Have you been outside the United States?"

"Paris. But the stars are the same as here. Too many lights to see them all."

"Make Rian take you somewhere. I'm not sure there's a place he hasn't been yet."

She shot him a half-smile. "You know damn well I'm not going to make Rian do anything."

Mara expected a witty comeback from Cathal. Instead, he hummed a few bars of a song she didn't recognize. "I don't think that's true, Mara. Neither Brogan nor I can make Rian do a damned thing. Selena has a little more pull with him, but you, darling, might be the grace he needs. You proved that today."

His cryptic comment bothered her. Along with Selena's questions about how serious they were. They both seemed scared or nervous for Rian. Rian had avoided some of her questions, as well. The small shifts in his body language.

The inconsistencies should make her back away, not get so attached.

"Something has driven me crazy today. I've asked Rian, but he won't tell me. What does his tattoo mean?"

Cathal's shoulders stiffened, similar to the reaction from Rian.

"*To the waters and the wild, with a faery, hand in hand*." Mara sighed. "I looked it up and came up with a hundred different theories."

"I'm afraid that your theories would be off the mark. But that's not my place to say. The most I can tell you is that Rian lived through something that changed him forever. But we all have, haven't we?"

"Yes." Shane had changed her. For the better, having come out on the other end of the relationship. She was stronger than his memory. Rian had made her realize that.

"My brother will tell you when he's ready." They stopped at her car, and Cathal opened her door. "But if you care for my brother, don't give up on him. I'm afraid things may get worse before they get better."

She didn't respond. Didn't have a clue what it meant. It seemed everyone in the world knew of Rian O'Keeley. He didn't need her more than she needed a dandelion. Here one day, gone the next. She wanted longer with him, but she wouldn't cover her eyes and pretend they'd be together forever.

But their relationship couldn't be one-sided. Not when whatever he hid was laced with so much pain. She cared too much to walk away.

She drove to her apartment and sat in front of the building. It seemed stupid, wanting more from a man like

Rian. She'd end up getting hurt in the end. Diving in, feet first, and suffering the consequences of risking her heart was worth it.

She put the car in reverse and pulled out of her complex, turning toward Rian's condo. She'd take Cathal's advice. While Rian was in her life, she wouldn't give up on him.

On their relationship.

RIAN SAT on the edge of the bed, watching Mara. He'd been with women all over the world, but never in his condo in Atlanta. He'd never been that relaxed to let someone slip-in this close to his true self. A part of him trusted her deeply. And someday he might be at a point he could tell her just that.

But it wasn't the time.

She might knock him upside the head with her flip flop the way she glared at him.

She looked frazzled and stressed and so damn cute he almost tugged her back into his bed. That's where he liked her at the moment, tightly tucked against his side and ignoring his responsibilities. Sneaking out after sex wasn't something that happened often, but it happened. It was usually a conscious decision for Rian to stay until morning.

With Mara, he wanted to stay. Wanted *her* to stay.

He knew he'd miss her when she left.

Mara stopped in the middle of his room, hands on her hips, wearing her jeans and a blue bra the color of the ocean. "I don't know what you think is so funny, Rian O'Keeley. I'm not worried about being late to my job, I'm worried about my mom showing up, and I'm still here in the same clothes I wore yesterday. She'd notice, too. Don't think she's one of those sweet Southern women that wouldn't call you out and risk being impolite."

"I'd never dream it."

She huffed and tossed a pillow in his direction. "You're useless."

"You didn't think so a few hours ago."

She bent her face away from him as she continued to search for her shirt, but he caught her smile. He made her happy.

That made him happy.

And, instead of reaching for her, he ran a hand over his hair. "Calm down. I told your mom nine. It's only eight-fifteen."

"Yes, but my mom is always early."

"Then I suppose you should put your shirt on."

She paused, straightened, and shot him a look. "Oh, *great* idea, Rian. Maybe if you helped me look for it—"

The doorbell rang.

Mara's eyes widened, and she took a big, deep gasping breath.

Rian stood and picked up the comforter from where it'd ended up on the floor, spotting the corner of her blue shirt from under the bed. "Here you are."

She snatched it from him. "She is going to kill me!"

He kept his laugh quiet as he left the room. Opening the door, he was surprised to see Selena.

"Are you alright? The baby?"

"I'm fine." Selena grimaced and stepped into his condo. "I know this probably isn't my place, but I'm concerned. We need to talk about Mara and the kid's thing."

"What about me?" Mara stepped out of the bedroom. "And kids?"

Rian swallowed over the tight, constricting feeling in his

throat. The peaceful morning disintegrated. Kids were off the table. He'd not told Mara yet, but her opinion on the subject didn't matter. It made him sound like a jackass to say that aloud, so he kept his mouth shut, waiting on his busybody sister-in-law to make the next move.

Selena turned pale, her mouth dropping open. Brogan would kill him if Selena passed out.

"Come in and sit." He took her by the elbow to the kitchen table. "And we're not talking about that. Not today."

Mara stood at the door to his condo, looking ready to run for it before her ma showed up, but waiting on someone to answer her. He didn't blame her. He'd want to know what the hell was going on as well.

"I don't like thinking I'm going to be the topic of conversation once I leave the room."

Rian shot a soft look at Selena, not wanting to upset her further, before crossing the room to Mara. "You and I have things to talk about, but I can't do it now. But it's talking about me that Selena wants, not you."

"Is it the same thing you couldn't talk about Saturday night?"

"Yes."

Her eyes narrowed as her lips pressed into a tight light, probably holding in the dozens of questions buzzing around her intelligent mind. "Alright. I'll leave because as much as I'm curious what you're keeping from me, I'm more afraid of my mother."

He crossed the floor and kissed her. "Thank you."

"But I want to know, Rian. I don't like feeling like there's a huge side of you that you're hiding. Not when you know everything about me."

He nodded, unable to promise anything. Mara should know about his past. About his future plans. They had a direct effect on her now, but he couldn't foresee when he'd be in a good state of mind to tell her the entire story and not crumble. She didn't need to see that side of him.

He couldn't acknowledge how fragile that far edge of his emotions still felt. It'd been well over a decade since his daughter died.

Rian stood at the door another few moments after she left, gathering himself to handle Selena with care. He wasn't mad at Selena. She was there to help.

"Rian?"

He turned, not realizing she stood so close.

"I'm sorry."

"Don't." He squeezed her shoulder and walked into the kitchen. "It's not your fault."

"She wants kids. That's what I wanted to tell you. I didn't say anything to her, but I didn't want you to be taken off guard by that."

"Thanks." He flipped on the coffeemaker and pulled down a cup. He'd assumed she wanted kids. "Do you want some tea, Selena?"

"No. I need to head into the restaurant. I didn't tell Brogan that I was coming here. He'd have stopped me." She tried to smile, but it still seemed sad. "Maybe he'd have been right."

"I run from my past. I'll never deny that. I've watched Cathal long enough to know that we're the same in that personality trait. I don't have any plans on marrying Mara or having children. This is the longest and closest I've gotten to one woman in over ten years. I'd just hoped to enjoy it a little longer before telling her, is all." Because she'd walk away. Mara was meant for marriage. She'd make an amazing mother. "I suppose I've been self-centered about the whole deal."

"And that personality trait you share with both your brothers. I'm not here to tell you how to handle this situation. I have no frame of reference, and my opinion isn't worth a damn, but don't throw away love before you give her a chance to make her own decision."

"I never said—"

"That you were in love?" She smiled brighter. "This wouldn't hurt you so badly if you weren't."

Selena walked out of his condo, leaving him with another giant ocean to navigate.

19

Mara gave Blair a high-five. "You are doing amazing! I'm so proud of how well you've learned math."

Blair wiggled in her seat, her gap-toothed smile full and bright. "Does this mean I get a special surprise?"

"Absolutely. I'll bring it tomorrow." Mara looked up as the door to the after-school center opened. Her mom and dad unexpectedly stepped into the lobby. It was nice they took the time on their way out of town to visit with her. Sometimes, she hated living so far away from them.

Her mom had spent the past two days side-by-side with Rian in his kitchen, neither one of them giving any details on what they'd made or created. All she knew was that her mom was pleased with Rian, and Rian was happy.

She'd count her blessings.

"Mom," she began as she moved across the gym floor, narrowly avoiding being hit by a dodge ball. "Boys! Cool it."

The boys mumbled and muttered, but they stopped playing long enough for her to pass by. "Hey! Are y'all headed out?"

"Yes." Her mom kissed her cheek. "I wanted to see you

one more time. It feels strange, coming all this way and spending more time with your boyfriend than with you."

Mrs. Peterson walked up from her office, her smile frozen in place. "You must be Mara's parents? Hi, I'm Laura Peterson." She shook hands. "And I didn't realize you had a boyfriend."

It was as if the world slowed down when her mom spoke. Heat burst in Mara's chest. She shook her head, but her mom was too damn proud of Rian to keep it inside.

"She's dating a famous chef, actually. He's the sweetest man. So driven and focused."

Mrs. Peterson crossed her arms. "Really? The same one who volunteered at the center?"

"Yes, I believe so." Her mom smiled. "Did you get a chance to meet him?"

"I did. I also warned your daughter that she'd consider herself out of the running for this position if she pursued a relationship with him." Mrs. Peterson shook her head, her fluffy, blond hair not daring to move. "I'm sorry, but I will have to include this in my report. And I came over here to tell you that the board of directors will announce a position in the next two weeks." Her chin tilted in the air. "And with my report, expect them to hold open interviews for the position now. There are other qualified candidates."

Mara stared at Mrs. Peterson. What could she say? Asking her, "what the hell was her problem," wasn't going to get her any brownie points, although it'd sure as hell make her feel better.

Her mom, on the other hand, didn't seem to have the same reservation. Her mom's eyes hardened until they were narrow slits. Mara took a small step back. It was like someone pulled the pin from a hand grenade. Dangerous.

Explosive.

Her dad stepped back as well.

"You *warned* her to stay away from Rian? Tell me, did my daughter do anything inappropriate while at work?"

Mara thought back to the almost kiss in the hallway.

Mrs. Peterson tilted her chin up. "Not that I'm aware of."

Oh, and the incredible kiss in the parking lot.

"Then, I don't see how it's your business who my daughter dates outside this facility."

"It's the appearance—"

Her mom held up her finger, cutting off Mrs. Peterson.

Mara looked past her mom to her dad. For once, he didn't look bored but looked like he might laugh at any moment.

"My daughter works her butt off for these kids. She's loving, dedicated, and the best person you could possibly hire to take over. Maybe the circumstances of her and Rian's meeting weren't perfect in your book, but they're in love. In my opinion, since that's the outcome, it doesn't matter when or how they met. They should be thankful to have found one another."

Mara swallowed over the thought of loving Rian. She loved him. Her mom knew. Did she genuinely think Rian loved her in return?

Had he said something?

Mrs. Peterson gave her mom and dad a curt nod. "I hope you both have a pleasant ride back to Alabama." She gazed at Mara. "I'm leaving at five-thirty today, so you'll need to close up."

"Alright."

The three of them stood there, watching the director walk away, still silent until she closed her office door.

Mara's mom patted Mara's back. "It'll work out, honey."

Mara shook her head. "Which part? Me and this job or me and Rian?"

"Both."

She hoped so. "Y'all get on the road. I'm going to finish up with Blair and then clean up." She kissed and hugged them goodbye and walked back to Blair to contemplate what to do with her life.

Because it was a life decision.

If she didn't get the job, she wouldn't have a choice but to leave the center. Her bank account, skipping by with barely enough for groceries, wouldn't last the rest of her life with two part-time jobs. She needed something more substantial. More permanent.

The rest of the day flew by, her mind halfway focused on the kids, and the other half on Rian. It was too late to call off their relationship to save her job. Not after the way her mom had laid it out for Mrs. Peterson. And she wouldn't walk away from Rian for her career, anyway.

She loved helping kids, and she'd find another job, but Rian was a once in a lifetime kind of man. Something still kept him at a distance, and that bothered her. Maybe she needed to push him a little more?

Not that she'd lump Rian in with her kids at the center, but sometimes, they needed the push. Blowing people off was what they excelled at. It seemed, for whatever reason, that Rian ignored whatever the issue was that he kept locked away from her.

She didn't want a one-sided relationship. She'd already warned him.

She walked into O'Keeley's a little after seven. Their dinner crowd was heavy for a Tuesday night. She waved to Katie, passed by the bar, and paused at the office door. She could do this. She could be a part of someone's life this way.

His friends and family started to become like her own. It scared her, to risk so much of herself, but Rian was worth it.

She knocked twice and waited.

Rian answered the door. "I knew it had to be you. No one else ever knocks." He stepped back and motioned her inside. His mood was light, and he seemed happy.

"I take it the time with my mom went as well as she said it did?"

"Absolutely." He kissed her. "How was your day?"

She shrugged. Getting into the situation with Mrs. Peterson would only drag down his mood. "Fine."

He watched her for a long moment, but he didn't ask another question.

"How was Romeo?"

"Great. One of the line cooks has made it his goal to teach him how to cook the perfect hamburger. Romeo enjoys eating as much as cooking." He gripped her elbow lightly. "Are you sure you're alright?"

"Mara, come see the ultrasound of the baby." Selena waved a black and white picture from where she sat on the sofa, giving Mara an excuse to avoid the question. "They hope to tell us in another week or two if it's a boy or a girl. I'm taking a special test to find out."

Cathal leaned up and grabbed his glass of whiskey from the table. "Why, don't you want it to be a surprise? Find out the way God intended."

"Because I want to pick out colors and names."

He waved his hand at Selena. "I have the names picked out for you."

She passed off the picture to Mara and crossed her arms. "Oh, really? And what has his or her fun-loving uncle decided?"

"Fun-loving?" Rian stepped beside Mara, his hand

resting possessively on her hip. "Is he the only uncle that gets that title?"

"I'll take the good-looking uncle. I like that title, too," Cathal said. "Smart uncle. Charming uncle."

"Conceited uncle," Rian interjected.

Mara stared down at the sonogram of Selena's baby. It was a blob. Cute, but still a blob. Her own quick wish for a baby surprised her. Selena had mentioned something about Rian and kids. He'd never elaborated like he said he would.

Not having children wasn't a deal-breaker, but it was hard to comprehend that a man as caring as Rian wouldn't want a child of his own. She understood some people didn't want kids. Her brother, Bennett, had sworn off kids as long as she could remember. And after seeing him as an adult, a focused police detective married to his job, Mara understood.

Mara held up the picture to Rian. "Did you see it?"

He barely glanced at it. "Yes."

Selena watched him cautiously, her eyes flicking to Mara's, before dropping to her lap.

Something was definitely up.

His thumb grazed along her skin, just underneath her shirt. His lips brushed her ear. "Stay with me tonight."

She wanted to.

He kissed her along the side of her neck.

No one in the room seemed to pay attention to him. That means they didn't notice how her eyes rolled back in her head as his warm breath trailed across her neck.

"Come home with me."

The word, "no," had escaped her vocabulary.

Selena shifted on the sofa and looked back at them, just as Rian straightened. "Oh, Mara, I forgot to tell you that your mom helped Romeo with his math homework today before she left town."

Mara blinked, trying to get her mind to function. Rian's body, the heat, size, pressed firmly against hers. A quick glimpse at him confirmed that he looked utterly at ease.

Unaffected.

Damn the man.

"No, I didn't know that. We didn't get much of a chance to talk."

Rian leaned away. "She said she'd stop by your work to say goodbye."

"She did." The entire room quieted down as if listening to her response. Odd to have that many people interested in what she had to say. "But, well, Mrs. Peterson overheard mom say something about you."

"And?"

She twisted her lips to the side, unable to even laugh it off. "It went about how you'd imagine."

Cathal sat down in the leather chair. "I have a poor imagination, so why don't you elaborate?" He held up his glass of whiskey. "What did your Mrs. Peterson say?"

Rian released her, crossing his arms. "I can only assume."

Brogan sat down next to Selena, his arm around her shoulders. "This is interesting."

"What?" Rian asked, cocking his head toward his brother.

"The idea of this Mrs. Peterson puts the same look on your face as the food critic does."

Mara rested her hands on the back of the sofa, leaning on it. "Mrs. Peterson is my boss. She's leaving in a couple weeks and has yet to name her replacement. She told me once I was forbidden from dating Rian. Then my mom let it out that we were together, and here we are." She threw her hands up before slipping them into her back pockets. "I'm waiting to be either fired or denied the promotion because of it. And they are opening the job up for external interviews."

Rian muttered something. Brogan pressed his lips in a firm line.

Cathal held his glass up. "Well, now, that sounds like some straight shit."

The room was silent for a half-beat before Selena snorted.

Brogan looked down at her. "I truly hope our child doesn't inherit that."

Rian shook his head, either at Brogan or Cathal, but Mara smiled. "You know what? It is shit."

Cathal grinned. "That's the spirit."

"I'll go talk to her." Rian rolled his shoulders the way he did when he was gearing up to face a challenge. Did he realize he did that? "Maybe she'll listen to reason."

Mara laid her hand on his arm. The muscles contracted. "Don't worry about it. I love the center and my kids, but I can find a job." She blew out a harsh breath. "Not many people are willing to work for peanuts."

"And live off frozen dinners," Rian muttered. He rubbed a hand over his head. "I'd hate you not getting that job because of me."

She'd hate it, too, but it wouldn't be because of Rian. She was the one that ignored Mrs. Peterson's dumb warnings. She'd chased him as much as he'd pursued her.

He lifted his head. "Come home with me tonight, Mara."

Selena tucked her head down low over the sonogram picture, probably feeling awkward having the invitation issued in front of everyone. Brogan avoided eye contact.

Cathal watched Rian, his face serious.

She didn't feel pressured. She easily could have sidestepped, claimed she was tired, vowed she had an early morning with work. But she wanted Rian. And he needed her.

He might not say those exact words, but he did. Cathal's worried glance confirmed that everyone in the room knew something she didn't. She had plenty of patience with the kids she worked with, but it was running short with Rian and whatever his secret might be.

20

"What do you want, Mara?"

Rian meant it in the most straightforward way possible. She'd mentioned that she was hungry at O'Keeley's before they left, and he'd planned to make her something to eat. A sandwich. An omelet. Something quick and easy. Anything to keep his racing mind off Selena.

Seeing Selena's baby, hearing that he or she had a heartbeat of 155 bpm, made it too real. Brought back too many memories. Brogan was happy. Selena was happy.

Hell, he'd been just as happy after the shock when he'd learned of his daughter.

Why couldn't he just enjoy the happiness of a new child? His own family? He opened a beer as he waited for Mara's answer. He had to separate his past with his family's future. Everyone in the room had noticed his sullen reaction, no matter how hard he tried to cover it up.

Mara's physical presence, pressed against his side, had kept him from coming unraveled.

She sat on the barstool at the counter, watching him with an unreadable expression.

Rian leaned against the counter wearing a pair of sweatpants, bare feet, and no shirt, meeting her eyes. The mood was too heavy between them. "I can make some whipped cream and grab the chocolate syrup, and we can head back to my bedroom if you're wanting something sweet."

Instead of smiling, she bit her lower lip. His blood started to hum. Damn, but the woman drove him crazy.

"You told me you'd explain what Selena had said before about kids. I can tell tonight bothered you. You wouldn't even look at the sonogram."

He pushed off the counter. He didn't have high expectations that she'd let it go, forget about the entire thing, but he'd wished it. He grabbed his beer and walked back to the bar, sitting down on the stool beside her.

"I can tell you don't want to talk about this, but I can't be with someone that makes me feel like they're hiding something."

He took a drink, trying to figure out how to say as little as possible. He wanted, no, needed her. Not pity. Not sympathy. Tonight, he needed her to simply be with him and push the thoughts and fears away.

Because he did fear for Selena and Brogan. Hell. He was scared for all of them living through it again.

He wished he could compartmentalize it like he used to, but Selena was too close to the family.

So, he decided to take the cowards way out and not give Mara full disclosure on his past. He would. Eventually. Maybe after his niece or nephew was born and fear didn't suffocate him.

"Why was Selena concerned about me and having kids the other morning?" She set her hand on his knee. "Why did you look so distant tonight?"

"The answer to that is the same. I can't have kids, Mara."

Her eyes widened. Her hand tightened where it lay on his leg. But she had no other response. She didn't ask him the reason behind it, so he didn't share.

Keeping the rest of his past from her pulled at his soul. She deserved to know everything about him like he felt he knew about her, but he couldn't. Not yet.

That was the best he'd give her at the moment.

"Alright."

He raised his eyebrows. No way it was that easy. Not the woman who wanted to dissect every problem in the world. "Alright?"

"I'm not saying this to scare you off, but if we ever did make it to that point, you not being able to have kids won't change anything for me."

"It doesn't scare you off? I thought you wanted kids." She'd make an excellent mother. Because of his own incapacity to handle another tragedy, he'd take that away from her.

She leaned forward, laying a sweet kiss on his lips. "No."

He heard the words, but the sadness in her eyes confirmed that it did bother her. Once she understood the reason behind it, maybe she'd understand. Or perhaps she wouldn't, and then she would leave.

God, he should go ahead and end it, but he couldn't. Not when so much of who he was at the moment was tied up, tangled with her.

"I don't want to talk about it any longer." He rose and held out his hand. "Come to bed with me. I need you tonight."

She rose, her lips tilting into a wry smile. "I thought we had chocolate syrup involved."

He pulled her tight, his lips brushing along the curve of

her neck. "I'd rather play with whipped cream. Peaches and cream. That sounds like a good dessert to experiment with."

He felt her pulse beating under his lips.

"I've never done any of that before," she whispered.

"Let me make the whipped cream, and we'll see how you like it."

She chuckled. "Make? What? You don't have a can of it?"

He managed to look horrified. "No. I actually have the ingredients from when I cooked with your ma." He palmed the back of her head, sinking into a deep, mindless kiss. The slow heat building between them until he could think of nothing but her. That's what he wanted. The oblivion.

"Go to the bedroom. I'll be there in a second."

Her mouth dropped open. "You're really going to make whipped cream? That sort of ruins the spontaneity of it. You know, having to measure things and get out the mixer."

He patted her hip. "Go, before I change my mind and we start and finish this right here."

She took a step toward his bedroom. "That might be fun, too." She turned and walked away.

Rian spent five minutes mixing the ingredients. Five minutes of his mind racing between the woman in his bedroom and the lie he'd told her.

No. It wasn't a lie.

Part truth?

Either way, he needed to come clean eventually. He piled the whipped cream into a dish and walked to his bedroom.

Mara sat in the middle of his bed, already stripped down to her bra and panties, waiting on him.

He let his worry go. Worry for Mara leaving him. Fear for his brother's child. Nothing would interrupt his evening with Mara.

.   .   .

SOMETHING DIDN'T SIT RIGHT with her. Mara stepped out of Rian's shower. He'd gone to the gym, something she'd never seen him do before, and left her alone in his apartment. She wanted to snoop. But she knew she wouldn't find anything.

Rian had quickly announced he couldn't have children. There were several medical reasons for a man not being able to father a child. The physical limitation didn't bother her.

No. He'd given her the result without the back story.

That was what struck her as odd. *Why* couldn't he have children? Did he have an accident? As far as she knew, everything looked to be in working order in that department.

An illness?

Was it hereditary?

Nope. Rian had dropped his bombshell without so much as a hint to the reason. Which means he didn't want to give her one. Still hiding.

Mara dressed quickly, applied a little makeup, and went to wait in his living room. She had her job interview that afternoon and would swing by her apartment to change into a suit.

Letting the subject drop for the time being, even though it left a cold feeling over her skin, seemed like the best option. But why did he still hold back from her?

The door opened, and he came in, drenched in sweat, shirtless, and overall, looking sexy as sin.

"It's not fair for you to look at me that way, Amara, and already dressed for the day." He grinned as he stalked toward her. "Can I persuade you back into my bed?"

"I've already taken my shower."

"That's an even better location seeing as I need one myself."

She let go of her worry and laughed. "I don't need a second one."

He looked at his watch. "You took off the day for your interview, right?"

She knew where this was going and crossed her arms. "That doesn't mean I need to spend all day at your place. I do have a cat to take care of."

"One more hour." He leaned his hands on the side of his sofa. Sweat beaded at his temple. His hair was darker, his eyes bright. "Just one. It might give you luck for this afternoon?"

"Do you really think you getting lucky will give me luck in my interview?"

"I'm Irish. You know half our economy is built on our belief in luck." He snagged her hand and tugged her to her feet. "There's only one way to find out."

SHE WOULDN'T APPRECIATE his interference, but Rian had no intention of his relationship with Mara to prevent her from obtaining her dream job. That's why, about two hours before her interview time, he arrived at the after-school center to speak with Mrs. Peterson.

A quick phone call from Mara's mom pushed him into donning a suit and driving to the center. Lindsay Andrews came up with the idea for Rian to go and speak to the trustees in charge of the hiring process. He needed to clear her name.

He walked into the big gymnasium and headed straight to Mrs. Peterson's office.

"Excuse me?" A man, bald-headed and close to seventy, stepped out from a room to the right. "Can I help you? The center is closed this time of day."

"Yes. I'm here to speak to Mrs. Peterson about the job—"

"You're here to apply for the job?" The man smiled. "I'm Mr. Wrens. Right this way."

"No, I'm not. I do need to speak with the selection committee, though."

The long, narrow room held seven other men and women, including Mrs. Peterson. Rian managed not to tug at his shirt collar at the lack of air conditioning. It smelled stale and musty. Did they do that on purpose? It'd distract him horribly if he came to a job interview and began to sweat almost immediately.

As it was, Rian's nervousness was nonexistent. He was there for Mara.

Mrs. Peterson rose. "Mr. O'Keeley?"

"I found him wandering around on the basketball court," Mr. Wren said with a wry smile.

"I'm not here to apply for the position. I'm here to discuss an applicant. Amara Andrews."

The people in the room shuffled their papers. Everyone except Mrs. Peterson. "No need to look for the application. She's the one I said was not the right fit for this organization."

Rian kept his voice even and smooth. "Did you provide the details to these ladies and gentlemen as to why you felt that way?"

She tilted her nose in the air but remained silent.

A woman at the end smiled warmly at Rian. "I assume you know the circumstances?"

"Yes. I volunteered with the children a few times recently. I asked Ms. Andrews out." He rubbed a finger over his lips to keep from smiling. "Several times, actually. And she declined." He looked directly at Mrs. Peterson. "Because of this job."

Mrs. Peterson crossed her arms. "And I warned her. *Several times.*"

"And she believed you. It took a lot of convincing to get Mara to go on a date with me."

Mr. Wrens shook his head. "It is against our policy for members of our staff to become involved with our volunteers."

"I haven't been back to volunteer since I did take her on a date." He left out their kiss at Fiona's bar. "Does that policy extend for eternity?"

The man chuckled again. "No. I don't suppose it does. I see your point." He looked down at his stack of papers and then at Mrs. Peterson. "Can you please pass around Amara's application to the trustees? She was our first choice before your report."

Mrs. Peterson's mouth opened and then shut. Her eyes narrowed. "You may regret your decision if this is her tendency. Dating volunteers. Going against our policy."

The woman at the end of the table clasped her hands together. "You know, she does have a point. Ms. Andrews will be in charge of the budget and vetting volunteers. We need someone that doesn't cast any doubt on her integrity."

"As for vetting other volunteers, are you worried about her becoming involved with them?" Rian made eye contact with each member. At their subtle nods, he smiled, a slow curve of his lips that earned him an eye roll from Mrs. Peterson. "Amara is with me now. That's not a worry."

The woman at the end grinned.

Mrs. Peterson huffed. "I can't believe this," she muttered under her breath.

The smile dropped from Rian's lips, his accent thickening. "I can't believe that you're willing to cast Mara in such a negative light after how much she's done for the children here. She's devoted her life to serving children. She loves this center, and if she doesn't receive this job, I can guarantee that she'll find a place where her talents and dedication are appreciated."

He adjusted his suit jacket, buttoning the one button and letting his argument sink in as he got his frustration under control. A few of the members sat back, watching him with unreadable expressions. The man in the middle, Mr. Wrens, tapped his finger on the stack of applications.

"That has helped us tremendously. Thank you for coming down."

Rian inclined his head. "My pleasure."

"We didn't catch your name."

"Rian O'Keeley."

The same woman at the end looked shocked. "The chef?"

"Yes." He took a step backward. "I'd appreciate you not mentioning that I came to Amara."

"Absolutely," the woman said.

Rian left, strolling out of the center as quickly as he'd come in. He'd accomplished exactly what he'd intended to do. Mara deserved that job. He couldn't give her everything she wanted in life. Kids. Family. But he could give her the kids she loved. The job she loved.

And that eased some of the guilt still eating him inside.

21

The center felt strange without children running around. Mara could walk across the floor without having to duck and weave around a dodgeball game. It'd be like this daily if she got the job. Nine to six. All day.

Mara wanted it more than anything.

She wanted to be in charge of the kids. Their experiences. A tightness in her chest made her pause before going into the interview room. These kids, the ones she helped, maybe the only ones she ever had.

It would have to be enough. She loved Rian too much to end their relationship over that one aspect of her future. If she even had a future with him. He'd not said or done anything that made her think he had any intentions of walking away any time soon, but he'd done nothing to make it permanent between them.

She took a deep breath. Those thoughts wouldn't get her hired. She had to sell herself over and above whatever Mrs. Peterson said about her.

The door opened. Another woman, about her age, left

the room. Mara gave her a pleasant smile before Mr. Wrens, the head of the trustees, met her at the door.

"Ms. Andrews. Please, come in." He stepped back and allowed Mara to pass. "We've been looking forward to speaking with you most of the day."

Really? That was odd. Or maybe not. At one time, she'd considered herself the front runner. They had some part-time help, but no one that knew the ins and outs as she did.

The room was full. Several of the trustees smiled at her. A few didn't. Mrs. Peterson straight-out scowled. Why did she hate her so much?

"Good afternoon," Mara began. She sat down at the table, crossed her legs, and prepared to answer their questions.

It took an hour. Most of the questions she could answer. The woman at the end, with the wide smile, kept staring at Mara but didn't ask any questions.

"Well, Mara, I think—" Mr. Wrens looked around at the panel, everyone nodding "—we can safely ask if you'd like the position."

She sucked in a large breath and managed to control her voice. "I'd love to accept it."

"Great. The position will start in a week. Mrs. Peterson can show you anything you're not already aware of."

Mrs. Peterson glared at Mara. She didn't care. She had the position, and Mrs. Peterson couldn't take it away. Had she tried? Probably. But, apparently, it hadn't mattered.

Mara shook each member of the trustees' hands. The lady who'd not asked her any questions, Mrs. Wang, shook her hand and tilted her head to the side, watching Mara.

"I know I'm not supposed to say this, he asked us not to mention him coming down here, but I'd want to know."

"Who?"

Mrs. Wang glanced to the side and lowered her voice. "Your boyfriend made an appearance."

Mara blinked. "Rian?" He'd come there. Why? What he'd do?

"Yes! You know, I follow all the entertainment news. I've seen him in the tabloids. I've eaten at O'Keeley's several times. It's one of those things that makes my heart believe in love when I see someone like him with someone—"

She trailed off. Mara wasn't offended. She'd thought the same thing. But why had Rian come?

"Dear, don't take it the wrong way. You're very pretty. But Rian—"

"Is gorgeous." Mara shrugged. "I know. Doesn't make sense." Her fingers itched to pull out her phone, find out what he'd said to the trustees.

Mrs. Wang shook her head slowly. "I'm sorry. I know I'm not saying this right. Darling, Rian was your biggest supporter. He admires how much you've devoted your life to these kids. Seeing a man that could have any woman acknowledge such an important personality trait makes him so much more attractive." She patted her shoulder. "I'm happy for you."

She left Mara standing there, dumbfounded. Had Rian come because of what Mrs. Peterson had said? Had he come for some other reason? Did he think she couldn't get the job without him?

That didn't make sense. Mara angled her chin up, ready for the confrontation, as Mrs. Peterson headed her direction.

"I hope you understand I didn't ask Rian to come here."

Mrs. Peterson clasped her hands together. "Maybe not."

The woman Mara saw leave the interview earlier, poked her head back into the room. "Aunt Laura, are you ready?"

Laura Peterson. Mara's eyes widened. "This is your niece?" The woman who'd interviewed before Mara.

Mrs. Wang paused by the door, her happy expression from before gone completely. She'd figured it out as well. "All I can say is that I hope you enjoy retirement, Mrs. Peterson." She patted Mara on the shoulder again. "Good luck, honey. I look forward to working with you."

Fire flew through Mara. Mrs. Peterson almost cost her a job. Her dream job. It'd taken Rian coming to reassure the board that she was worthy.

Mara breathed through her nose, sounding a little like a dragon. "I will be back for my shift." She brushed her shoulder against Mrs. Peterson's and walked right out of the center. That woman. The nerve!

The drive to O'Keeley's was short, her mind never settling down. She pushed open the door, glad the crowd was light. She didn't recognize anyone, but Rian's car sat in the employee's parking lot, so she knew he was nearby. She checked the office first. Empty. So she headed to the kitchen.

Pushing the door open slowly, she peeked in. He stood there with a bowl full of peaches and the ingredients for whipped cream. It reminded her of their time together. Damn, that'd been a fun night. Was he really designing a dessert based on her, as he'd mentioned? Peaches with whipped cream.

That took a little steam out of her anger.

Oh, she wasn't angry with him. He'd basically saved her job. She was pissed off that women like Mrs. Peterson made it necessary to do so.

Rian looked up. "Over already?"

"Yes. Didn't take long." She stepped inside the door but still a few feet away from him. "Mrs. Wang told me about your visit."

He nodded, wiped his hands on a towel, and leaned on the counter. "I asked them not to. I didn't think it was fair, Mrs. Peterson trying to keep you from being hired because of us. And I'm partially to blame for it. I'm sorry if that angers you."

"No. I'm not angry with you. Thank you for going. It probably did help me get the job."

His quick smile shot straight to her heart. "That's wonderful!"

"Turns out Mrs. Peterson had an alternative agenda. It wasn't just me. Her niece had applied for the position."

He moved around the counter, gripping her shoulders in his hands. "You deserve that job."

She thought about what Mrs. Wang said. About Rian. About the way he valued her priorities. He looked at her like he loved her. He'd not said the words, but she felt it all the same. At a minimum, he cared for her.

She'd take that for the time being.

Rising on her toes, she kissed him. It wasn't passionate, not with about seven other people, cooks and waiters, buzzing around them, but she tried to show him she cared for him in return. Loved him.

"As sweet as this looks," Selena said from the doorway, one hand gripping her side, the other braced on the door frame. "I think I may need some help."

"What's wrong?" Fear like she'd never thought possible flashed across Rian's face before it disappeared. He truly cared for his sister-in-law.

"I don't know. It hurts." She sucked in another deep breath, sweat beading at her temple.

Rian jogged to Selena. Mara followed right behind him. "She needs to go to the hospital. Take her in my car." She shoved her keys into his hand. "It's easier to get out of."

He picked Selena up like a child as extreme panic crossed his features again.

They were close enough to the hospital that calling for an ambulance would have taken longer than driving her there. But there was no way Selena would feel comfortable riding in Rian's sports car. Getting her in and out would be nearly impossible with as low as it sat to the ground.

"Where's Brogan?" Mara asked, following them into the dining room.

"I already called him. He should be here soon." Selena squeezed her eyes shut and pressed her forehead to Rian's shoulder, mumbling, "Shit. Shit. Shit."

Cathal walked in the front door as they made it there. The smile fell from his face immediately. "What the hell?" He set a tentative hand on Selena's shoulder. "Darling?"

Rian pushed past him without explanation. Mara shoved Cathal along with Rian. "Selena's in pain. Rian's taking her to the emergency room. Call your brother and have him meet you there." She waved her hand in their direction. "Go."

Cathal jogged after Rian.

Mara turned around. The entire restaurant stared at her. The waitstaff. The customers. Mara checked her watch. She had two hours before she had to be at the center for after school. She'd hold down the restaurant until then.

But she needed help.

She walked to the hostess. "Who's managing right now?"

"Selena was," the girl, maybe nineteen, mumbled. Her eyes were wide with fear. Odd how young someone looks when they're scared.

"Alright. Do you have Katie's number?"

"Yes, ma'am."

After a pause, Mara sighed. "I need it."

The girl pulled out her phone and passed it to Mara.

Mara smiled gently over her anxiety. "Can you unlock it and call her? Ask her to come in."

"You want her to come in on her day off?"

"Yes."

"Do you think she'll listen to me?"

"Call her," Mara began, keeping her frustration out of her voice, "and I'll tell her to come in."

The girl didn't move. "Are you the manager now?"

She sounded like Blair with every response in the form of a question. "Call Katie and give me the phone," Mara finally snapped.

Katie answered on the second ring. "You're working, Taylor, why are you calling me?"

"Katie, this is Mara. I'm—"

"Rian's girlfriend. Yeah. What's up?"

"Selena went to the hospital."

There was paper shuffling and then a door closing. "Which hospital? Is Brogan with her? What does she need?"

"I don't know which hospital they went to. I know you want to see her, but I need help. Everyone left, and O'Keeley's is pretty much without anyone to run it." Mara could wait tables. She couldn't run a restaurant. "Can you come in and help?"

"Absolutely. Be there in fifteen." She hung up.

A sigh of relief washed through Mara.

Taylor tapped her on the shoulder. "Um, Katie isn't a manager."

"She is today."

Taylor bit her lower lip. "I'm not sure Mr. O'Keeley will like you taking over."

She almost responded that she was sleeping with one of the *Mr. O'Keeley's* but decided to keep that to herself. "For the time being, Katie is in charge. If Mr. O'Keeley doesn't like it, then he can fire me. I'm sure you'll get better directions from Rian or Cathal soon, but for now, just assume that I can appoint someone in charge. And I picked Katie."

Taylor nodded but still didn't look convinced. Did Brogan and Selena run that tight an operation? Apparently.

22

The beeps of the machines. The smell. The way the nurses rushed back and forth. Rian hated all of it. Especially since he was in the hospital because of his niece or nephew. The doctor had found the heartbeat. It was strong. Steady. He'd even heard murmurs of it being a boy. But they were worried about Selena's contractions. If that's what they were, being so early in the pregnancy.

Rian had a hard time focusing on what'd happened. It was a blur now. His own memories threatened to break him apart. He wouldn't let them. Going over and over the new recipe in his head, the dessert he'd been making, at least a dozen times gave him something to think about.

And he wanted Mara there with him.

She anchored him. Just a touch of her hand or press of her body against his side seemed to chase away his fears. Worry. Anxiety. But she'd pushed them out of O'Keeley's to get Selena tended to. He appreciated her quick thinking. He'd stood there, watching Selena's face contort in pain, and did nothing.

A hand slipped over his shoulder.

He closed his eyes.

He knew her before he saw her face. "Mara." He turned, wrapping his arms around her, burying his face against her neck. Taking a deep breath, he let the peace she brought run over his skin. He wasn't this clingy. He'd set his life up to be alone. He was happy alone.

"I called one of those car companies to bring me. You didn't leave your keys."

He lifted his head, kissing her with every inch of emotion he felt. She didn't hold back, letting his lips move over hers rougher than expected. The feel of her mouth against his, the taste of her, eased the muscles along his shoulders.

Her lips curved up in a small smile when he lifted his head. "A few more minutes and you might have taught these nurses a move or two." She brushed her hand along his temple. "Are you alright?"

"I'm not worried about me. I'm worried about Selena."

"I know, I am, too. But I'm also worried about you. I saw Cathal outside. He said the doctor thinks the baby is fine. And so is Selena. But you look like you're about to break apart. So, what is it?"

He shook his head. "Nothing. Just worked up." He looked at his watch. "You're due at the center in twenty minutes."

She scrunched up her nose. "I know. I don't want to be late the first day I'm hired, but I wanted to check on you."

"Who's at the restaurant?"

"I put Katie in charge." She lifted a shoulder. "She's the only other person I know that works there."

He pulled her flush against his body again. He didn't care about the nurses or others in the waiting area. He needed her. Her heart.

"Thank you for caring about my family."

She laughed, softly and sweetly. "That's an odd thing to say. Why wouldn't I care about your family? They're yours, and I care about you."

He kissed her again. He didn't deserve her. Her trust. Not after she flat out asked him why he acted the way he did, and he'd withheld so much. He'd tell her. Tonight. Even if retelling it made him relive it all over again.

The competition was in three days. Clearing the air would help with his focus.

She pulled back. "Rian—" She waited, searching his face, probably expecting him to explain it. After a long silence, she stepped away. "Is there any way I can see Selena before I leave?"

"I'm sure." He interlaced his fingers with hers and led her down the hallway. A few nurses smiled at them and nodded.

A low murmur of voices in Selena's room made him pause. If the doctor were inside, he'd finish whatever type of exam they needed to do. He loved Selena like his own flesh and blood, but some things were too personal.

Mara seemed to understand because she didn't question it when he stopped.

Until Brogan's voice, deep and loud, spoke. "If it's upsetting you, then I'll send him back to the restaurant."

Selena replied, too low for Rian to hear.

"No," Cathal said, from somewhere just inside the room judging by the volume of his voice. "I disagree with you, Selena. Rian lost his own child. If he's not ready to face that head-on then who are we to push him? I'd resent you both if you did the same to me. Let him have his time. He'll process this the same as he always does."

"You lost a child?" Mara's expression shifted between shock and sadness. "Is that what you kept from me? Why?"

He took a step away from the door, sucking in a deep breath.

"Why wouldn't you tell me that?"

"I can't do this, Mara."

She reached out, but he backed away. He'd crumble. With his emotions frayed from Selena's emergency, he didn't have it in him to keep it together. Not right then.

Her hand fell to her side. "Do you need me to stay with you instead of going to work?"

"No. It'd be for the better for you to leave." Then maybe he'd have a chance to pull himself together.

"When you're ready to talk about this, about all of it, you know where to find me." She stepped to him and kissed him lightly on the cheek. When she pulled back, her eyes shining with tears. "Goodbye, Rian."

And for the second time in his life, his heart shattered as he watched her walk away.

The door to Selena's room opened. Cathal stood there, his eyes tired but sharp. "Hey there, brother. Did I hear you talking to someone?"

"Amara." Rian swallowed. "She left." He ran a hand over his hair. This wasn't happening. He sucked in a deep breath of air. "I'd like to see Selena. Then I'm going to head back to the restaurant." He swallowed over the pain of Mara. "Katie is in charge right now."

Cathal grimaced. "I may go back with you to help."

Rian finally ventured into the hospital room. Selena, looking healthier, sat upright in her bed. A blue and white hospital gown was partway snapped on her shoulder. An IV connected her to a bag of fluids. She poked her finger at the clear bag and halfway smiled. "Turns out, I'd dehydrated myself."

"Working too hard," Brogan mumbled. He leaned his elbows on the bed, his hands clasped around Selena's free hand. The man might never let her go. And Rian, for the first time ever, felt a pang of jealousy at their relationship.

Of his brother, for being able to live his life without the dark cloud following him everywhere.

Rian walked over, planted a kiss on the top of Selena's head, and then slipped his hands in his pockets. They were shaking. For Selena and the baby. For Mara. For himself.

He couldn't figure out what pain to focus on at the moment. It twisted around inside him like a destructive tornado. But his brothers didn't need his shit piled at their feet again. Not with the competition in a few short days.

Something that could push their restaurant to another level with the media coverage it'd started to garner.

"I'm headed back to O'Keeley's. I'll relieve Katie. I'm sure she'd like to come to see you."

Selena held up her phone. "She's texted me nonstop."

"Still working," Brogan said. "You're going to have to slow down."

She shot him an annoyed look.

"Just until everything evens back out again." He kissed the back of her hand. "You scared me."

Her eyes softened.

Rian looked over them at Cathal.

Cathal nodded, and they both said their goodbyes and left. Cathal kept a slow pace beside Rian, down the hallways, waving and possibly winking at a nurse as she passed by.

"Are you ready for Saturday?"

Rian shrugged. He couldn't focus. Not on that. He fingered Mara's keys in his pocket. He'd never given them back to her. Which means she had to call another ride to get to her job. He'd screwed up again.

Cathal nudged his shoulder. "What's your deal?"

He looked down at the ground. "Mara found out about..." He couldn't even say the words.

"Oh. Did you tell her all of it?" The shock in Cathal's voice made sense.

"No. I didn't explain anything, really. She told me goodbye and walked out. And now I gotta figure out what to do." Did he end it or commit? "I don't feel it's right to go to her and not be willing to lay it all out. I never wanted to put either one of us in this position."

"I'm sure Mara will understand your reluctance about having children."

He scratched the back of his neck, grimacing as he glanced at Cathal. "I told her I can't have kids."

Cathal held open the elevator door, his gaze locked on Rian. "That you *can't* have kids? But not the 'why' behind it?" Cathal whistled low. "And she just found out the rest of the story?"

"Partly."

Cathal set his hand on Rian's shoulder. "I hope you're planning on chasing after her."

"No. Not right now." He pushed his hands into his pockets. "I need to figure out my future with her. That's hard to do when my mind won't calm down and focus on one damn thing at a time."

"You need to get back in the kitchen. Cook. Create. Let it all settle down. Selena and the baby are alright. And until you can make some clear choices about your future with Mara, focusing on winning the competition is the best thing you can do for her. Her program could use that money. The competition is in three days, and you need to figure out the dessert you'll make. You and Philip agreed to a three-course meal. Is Lindsay Andrews coming to help you Saturday?"

Rian cocked his head to the side. "Why would she?"

"Because I got an email, not ten minutes before this happened with Selena, that Philip requested one person to assist. I almost refused. If he can't cook in a kitchen alone and turn out a delicious meal like you can, then screw him."

"So, you haven't replied?"

The elevator opened, and they stepped off into the parking garage. "Nope. Wanted to ask you first, seeing as I'm not the one doing the cooking."

Mara might come to the competition if her ma was there. "Tell him, yes." Rian pulled his phone out as he walked to Mara's car. "I'm going to call her right now."

"Who? Mara?" Cathal paused beside his own car. "I'm not sure that's a conversation you should have over the phone."

"No. Mrs. Andrews."

23

Mara opened her door to leave, to go anywhere but stay in her cramped apartment waiting around for Rian. She'd done that the past few days and hadn't heard a thing from him. His competition was today.

"Mom?" Her mother stepped off the elevator, wearing jeans, white sneakers, and a gray O'Keeley's T-shirt. "What are you doing here? Dressed like that?"

"I'm cooking with Rian." She held her hands out in a cute pose. "How do I look?"

Mara laughed, although the mention of Rian caused a ripple of stomach cramps. She'd had them since she'd walked away from him at the hospital. She'd wanted to turn around a dozen times and tell him everything was alright.

But she knew it wasn't.

"I came to pick you up." Her mom held the elevator door open. "Let's go."

"I...I hadn't decided if I was going or not. I'm not sure where Rian and I are in our relationship."

"That's why I'm here."

She waited for the elevator doors to close. "Did Rian tell you to come and get me?"

"No. He told me the two of you were working through something. Other than that, the man's been tight-lipped." She slipped a hand around Mara's waist. "Honey, that man looks like he's been put through hell." She brushed a strand of hair away from Mara's face. "And you do, too."

"That's not much of a compliment."

Her mom squeezed her again and let her go. "It wasn't meant to be a compliment. Every couple goes through hard times. You grow together, or you grow apart. You and Rian were intense so quick; there was bound to be a point where you both had to pause."

It was a little more than a pause, as her mom called it. Rian had kept a massive part of his past hidden from her. The tattoo on his back made sense after the revelation that he'd lost a child. He'd hurt her more by telling her the half-truth that he couldn't have kids.

"Stop huffing like a five-year-old, Amara." Her mom walked out of the elevator ahead of her. "You can't fix your problems if you hide away from them."

"I know that, but I wasn't going to bring it up. Not today. Rian needs to concentrate. If I'm there, I'm scared he won't be focused."

She opened the door in the lobby and waited for Mara. "That man is better with you. He knows it. And if you are a distraction, then maybe it will force him to face the problem. Because he's hiding from it, too."

"I don't need to distract him, Mom."

Her mom stopped her as she passed and cupped her face. "He needs to see that you haven't left. I know he told you he couldn't have kids, and I know you. I know your heart. That's not the reason for this fight."

"No. It's not." Not exactly, at least. Mara narrowed her eyes, trying to understand why her mother, of all people, would suddenly become a peacekeeper. "Why are you doing this?"

She walked to the driver's side of her car. "I don't want you to throw this relationship away. I came to Atlanta, expecting, planning," she smiled, but there was no warmth in her eyes, "hoping to lay into Rian O'Keeley for breaking your heart. Your father was glad to see me leave. Ever since you called and told us that you and he might have broken up, I've paced the house. And then Rian called. He'd sounded as cheerful as someone getting a root canal."

"What did he say about me?"

"Not a thing. Nothing. He only talked about the competition. What was at stake. So, I didn't bring it up. And I won't bring it up. But I can put the two of you in the same room. Get in the car, Mara."

Mara did as she was told, letting her mom drive her to O'Keeley's and not having a clue as to what to say when she saw Rian.

"You said something was at stake. What do you mean?"

"Did Rian not tell you what he gets if he wins today?"

"No. I didn't realize there was a prize besides pride for beating Philip."

Her mom exhaled. "Lord, you are in the dark on this. His pride is part of the prizes. If he loses, he has to mention Philip's restaurant in every magazine article, interview, anytime he talks about cooking, for the next year."

"He agreed to that? What was he thinking?" He despised that man. That would torture Rian to continually be reminded he'd lost.

"He thought to have Philip agree to donate twenty-five

thousand dollars to your after-school program should Rian win."

Mara gaped at her mother, unable to utter a sound.

He'd bet his prestige, his reputation, for her program to have money. Why? How could he care for her so much on the one hand and then not share something so life-changing? Did he not trust her? Maybe it was like she'd told herself since the beginning, nothing but a fling for Rian. He'd move on. Start traveling again. Find someone else to occupy himself with.

It'd just felt like more.

She stepped through the door at O'Keeley's, bracing herself for the rejection of even showing her face. Cathal stopped talking to a large man, cutting off the conversation abruptly and walking to Mara with his arms open wide.

"Mara! We've missed seeing you." He gave her a big hug.

She hugged him back, unsure of her next move. "Thanks?"

He pulled back, winked, which looked far more sinister than necessary, and led her over to the big man. "Philip, this is Mara. She's the director at the after-school program you'll be donating to."

Philip didn't smile. "You're the woman that Tiffany mentioned." He crossed his arms over his broad chest. "Right before she broke up with me. When I found out you were Rian's girlfriend, it made sense. You convinced her to end things."

Did he intend to look intimidating? If so, she didn't appreciate it. Not coming from the dumbass that treated Tiffany like crap and tried to ruin Rian's restaurant.

But big, dumb men trying to use their size to get her to do what they wanted didn't bother her. Not after Shane. She'd developed an immunity to it. Like allergy shots. She'd had so many instances with Shane that men like that all fell into the same, pathetic category.

Cathal set an arm over Mara's shoulders. "Philip here was just saying how he plans to humiliate Rian." He squeezed her shoulder. "*And* his assistant."

Mara's back straightened, and her eyes narrowed. Oh, that wasn't happening. Even Shane knew not to talk about her mother.

Philip barred his teeth. "Both of them will be the laughingstock of the culinary world once I'm through with them." He glanced around the room. "I figured he'd beg Pete to come work with him. Pete probably created the recipes anyway, letting Rian take the glory."

Mara shifted closer to the big doofus.

Cathal dropped his arm. And might have started to hum a happy tune. Her crosshairs were set on Philip.

She poked him in the chest. "You," she began, feeling every ounce of anger welling up inside toward the man. She poked him again, taking a step.

He stepped back.

"You do *not* get to come into Rian's restaurant and start insulting people. Pete isn't helping Rian. I don't even know who the hell Pete is." She pointed toward her mom, who stood to the side. "That is the woman assisting him. She's a wonderful cook who will help Rian kick your ass. Because she's amazing. And, unlike you, she has class. I didn't tell Tiffany to break up with you. I listened while she listed out every bad quality you possess. Which was a damn long list. That is why Tiffany broke up with you, you controlling, neurotic, manipulative dipshit!"

She caught a glimpse of Rian rushing in her direction. He wore a white chef's outfit and a baseball hat, and for some reason, it looked sexy on him.

Someone nearby took her picture. The comment her mom made, about her looking like hell, flicked through her mind. Great. She'd probably be on every gossip page as Rian's crazy girlfriend.

Probably ex-girlfriend based on the scowl on his face.

She shouldn't have come here.

The shock that registered on Philip's face after she'd called him a dipshit disappeared. If anything, he seemed larger. Towered over her. "You told her to break-up with me, didn't you?"

Cathal, who'd remained by her side, stepped away as Rian approached.

But Rian didn't stop to yell at her for disturbing the competition. He stepped in front of her, his arms crossed, blocking her as he'd done with Shane. Protecting.

"Back the hell up." Rian's deep voice, angry, sent a shiver down her spine.

Philip stood there another moment before holding his hands up and taking a step away. "I'll just kick your ass the way it counts. Then, you'll be my personal spokesperson for the next year."

Cathal chuckled, but it didn't reach his eyes. No, the youngest O'Keeley probably looked amused to most people there, but Mara saw it. He'd been ready to fight Philip.

Is that what Cathal wanted? Mara to cause some type of fight?

Philip walked away. A man, thin and short, rushed after him. Maybe his assistant?

Rian turned around. He didn't reach for her. His jaw bunched as his eyes skimmed over her face. "I'm sorry for him. Are you alright?"

"I'm fine."

"I didn't know if you'd show up or not."

She hitched a thumb over her shoulder. "My mom didn't give me a choice."

"I'm glad you're here, even if you don't want to be."

She hesitated. Did he really want her here? "I didn't want to distract you."

"Not having you here would have been more of a distraction." He shifted closer.

Now wasn't the time to discuss it. She tilted her face to his. The storm in his eyes almost broke her.

"Please stay for the competition." He lifted her hand to his lips, kissing the back of it.

"I will. I'm here for you."

Rian leaned down, giving her the lightest, sweetest kiss she'd ever received. And she hoped like hell it wasn't their last kiss.

"I need to get ready," he murmured.

She nodded, unable to speak. It hurt to love him. Not for his lying, but for the dread that he wouldn't make it right. And the fear that her love was one-sided.

Or he'd walk away instead of moving closer.

Her mom stepped up beside Rian. "I'm proud of the way you stood up to that man." Then her eyes narrowed, and Mara knew she was in trouble. "Next time, I'd appreciate you keeping your words clean. I didn't raise you to speak that way."

"Yes, ma'am." She hugged her mom. "Good luck."

"Thanks, baby."

Without overthinking, Mara hugged Rian as well. His long arms wrapped around her, holding her tight against his body. She blinked back the same damn tears that threatened to fall since walking out of the hospital.

She kept her face averted as she slipped out of his embrace. "I'll see you later."

"Alright."

"Let's go," her mom said, gently pushing Rian toward the kitchen.

As soon as they left, Mara found herself flanked on either side by O'Keeley's.

Selena linked her arm with Mara's. Cathal stood on the other side. Selena spoke first. "Come to the office."

They led her through the crowd of thirty, nearly forty people and into the office. Dozens of photographers took pictures of Selena, Cathal, and Mara as they hurried to the office.

"No wonder Rian likes to stay low key when he's home," Selena said, releasing Mara as soon as the office door shut behind them. "I've retouched my makeup twice, but I still look a hot mess. I'm all swollen from the IV bags at the hospital." She sat back on the sofa with a groan. "My hips hurt, and my pants wouldn't button today." She waved both hands in the air. "Yay for being pregnant."

Mara smiled at her. "Not just being pregnant, but now someone is taking your picture each time you leave the office. Sounds like a nightmare."

"Excuse me, ladies." Cathal walked into the bathroom, a T-shirt in his hand

"It's a nightmare." She leaned forward. "But are you alright? I know something is going on between you and Rian."

"I hope we'll be fine. That's really up to Rian." She'd already forgiven him. He needed to make up his mind about their relationship.

Selena blew out a tense breath. "I know the feeling. Do you want to talk about it?"

Mara shook her head. Because if she started, the tears she'd been fighting would finally fall.

Cathal emerged, wearing an O'Keeley's shirt and pair of dark wash blue jeans.

Mara smiled. "Wow. You look different like that."

He held his arms out. "Bad?"

"No." Selena laughed. "Not bad."

Brogan came into the office. His smile dropped. "What the hell are you doing?"

Cathal checked his watch. "Leaving you to wear a suit for the day. I'm going to help in the kitchen. Washing and such. I'd have looked a little odd wearing a suit. They're supposed to start cooking in ten minutes."

"Do you think the judges are settled?" Mara asked, needing something to do to keep her mind off Rian. "I can go see to them if you'd like a moment off your feet."

Selena leaned forward to stand up, but Brogan stepped into her way. "That'd be wonderful, Mara. Thank you. Selena will be out once the competition starts."

Selena crossed her arms and huffed, sitting back.

Cathal held the door open for Mara. "The judges are sitting over there, where we usually have the band on Saturday night."

"I'm on it."

Cathal hesitated. "I'm sorry about earlier. I knew Philip would be a jerk once he knew who you were, and I also knew that Rian wouldn't tolerate it, but I didn't know Philip would act so aggressively. I'd never put you in that situation on purpose. And I was right there if anything happened."

"I know. Thanks. He's a moron, and I'm glad Tiffany broke up with him."

"I think you called him a self-centered dipshit." Cathal smiled. "Let's hope Rian wins today. No one will be able to live with Rian for the next year if he's forced to laud the praises of the arse."

"He really shouldn't have bet that."

"Why? He knows he'll win. And because the stakes are so high for him, he made Philip put his own money up in return." Cathal nudged her shoulder with his. "For you, no less." He laid his arm around Mara's shoulders and squeezed. "Like I said before, don't give up on him. Things were bound to get worse before they get better."

Cathal left her at the kitchen door, and Mara turned and focused on the judges instead of Rian. They couldn't do anything about it for the next few hours, at least.

The three judges stood near the entrance. Two men and a woman. She recognized one name. It was the same as a restaurant on the other side of downtown Atlanta. Fancy and gourmet. Not a place she and Rachel would have ever ventured.

The other man was young. Twenty-two? Twenty-three? He smiled at her as she approached and held out his hand.

"I'm Casey," he said with an Australian accent. "You're the lady who just yelled at Philip, right?"

Because *that* was the title she wanted to carry around all day. "Yeah. Sorry about that. If you'd like to follow me—"

"No need to apologize." Casey grinned, revealing a dimple in his cheek. He reminded her of a lead singer in a boy band. Perfect hair and white teeth. "I enjoyed watching the show. Did I correctly hear that you're Rian's girlfriend?

She nodded and motioned to the table a second time. "Right here—"

"I've always admired the beautiful women Rian dates." His eyes sparkled. Literally, it looked like one of his blue eyes twinkled at her. "Let me know if you'd like to go out sometime."

"What part of 'girlfriend' confused you?" God, she was old enough to have babysat this kid.

He chuckled, unaffected by her tone. She needed to get it together and not offend the judges. That wouldn't help Rian win.

"I just know Rian's tendency toward hopping from woman to woman. I figured the women he dated knew that as well."

She put her hands on her hips. Before she could tell off the brat, the female judge stepped forward. Her gray hair was styled elegantly in a twist, and she had on bright red lipstick. With the hot pink sequins on her shirt and big, chunky gold jewelry, she looked like a Las Vegas grandma.

"Ignore Casey. I'm Virginia Lansing." Her smooth, Southern accent sounded as though she might come from Mississippi. "Do you mind if I get a water?"

Finally, something to do. "Yes. Absolutely. Does anyone want anything else while you wait?" She held up her hand in front of Casey's face when he opened his mouth and stepped closer, that damn twinkle there again. "To drink or to eat?"

Virginia chuckled. The other man ordered a coffee. Casey asked for a beer.

Fine. She could do that and then avoid Casey and his annoying twinkles. She had enough to worry about at the moment.

24

R ian prepped the peaches. Lindsay Andrews worked alongside him. She'd been amazing. Hardworking. A calm voice of reason when the first batch of salmon he'd cooked stuck to the bottom of the pan because he'd rushed. It was almost as though his own Ma had appeared through Lindsay.

"What made you want to do a peach cobbler?"

Rian thought of Mara. And of the whipped cream.

"That's the first time you've smiled all day." Lindsay leaned her hip on the counter and crossed her arms. "Tell me."

He couldn't go into much detail, but he'd tell her the inspiration. "Your daughter." He tucked his head down. "She smells like peaches."

"Oh my." Lindsay continued peeling the ripe peaches, the juice running across the cutting board. "That is something."

Rian set the sliced peaches into a bowl and set it aside. The rest of the peaches he'd blend into a puree.

"Rian, tell me, have you told my daughter you love her?"

He hesitated, pausing as he measured sugar. "No."

"Do you plan on it?"

He wanted to shift the conversation away from Mara. He still hadn't figured out what to do. The thought of Mara walking out of his life scared the shit out of him. And the fact it scared him, tripled the feeling.

Lindsay set a hand on his shoulder. "Honey, what is the one thing about Mara that bothers you?"

He looked at the woman. "That's not a usual question. Normally, people ask you what you like most about a person."

Lindsay smiled and resembled Mara so much it made him take a deep breath.

"Yes. I suppose they do. But this is Mara. I know my daughter. She's sweet and caring. She's made a huge sacrifice by wanting to work with underprivileged youth. You and I both know she has a million good qualities. I assume your trouble isn't because of those?" She tilted her head to the side, watching him. "Unless she's too good for you?"

Philip was on the other side of the kitchen, shouting orders at his assistant.

Rian's assistant was giving him a life lesson.

"No. I mean, yes. Mara is too good for me. But her qualities are all something I admire." Those were what made her different from all the women he'd dated in the past. She was selfless.

"Then, what is it, Rian?"

Philip laughed from his station across the kitchen. "What the hell? Giving up already, Rian? You know your food doesn't have shit on mine."

The shift in Lindsay Andrews's face made him take a

step out of the way. He'd seen that fury enough times in Cathal's.

She spun around, slapped a hand on the countertop, and stared down Philip. "You can leave this kitchen unless you keep that foul language out of your mouth."

Philip still had a cocky smile on his face. "Look, lady—"

"I ain't your lady, boy. Clean it up, shut your mouth, or leave. Those are your only options."

Philip looked past her to Rian. "Is she seriously going to kick me out of your kitchen."

"Yes." No way he'd go against Lindsay at that moment. His Ma would have done the same thing.

Philip mumbled something and went back to his workstation.

Lindsay turned around, picked up a knife, and sliced another peach. "Now, you were about to tell me what about my daughter is causing this issue?"

Rian pulled the blender out from underneath the counter and started to load the peaches into it. It wasn't one specific thing, one argument or one fight; it was Mara being —well, Mara.

He leaned on the counter, head down. "She pushes me." Part of him loved that about her, and part of him resisted. His brothers had let him handle things his own way. And he'd ran. And ran.

Stopping in one place, staying with Mara, meant facing down his past and dealing with it.

Lindsay motioned to the spacious kitchen. "It seems as though you're used to pushing yourself. You wouldn't have been this successful otherwise."

Rian shook his head. "No. It's not that, although her pushing me to create something in the kitchen was hard to swallow. She wants to know about my past."

"Aw. I see."

"You do?" He waited while Lindsay loaded her peaches into the blender.

"A woman wants to know about who she's with. Besides being someone for you to confide in, you're dating a woman with a degree in psychology. Believe me, she's already analyzed you five hundred different ways."

"Oh, I know." He walked to the sink and washed his hands. "She probably has a million questions when it comes to me. I'm just not sure how to give her the answers."

He turned around. Lindsay, her expression unreadable, crossed her arms. "What are you afraid of? Does being with Mara scare you?"

He swallowed over the lump that suddenly formed. "Living without your daughter scares me."

"And you think, once you explain your past, she'll leave?"

"No." She wouldn't leave. He understood Cathal's reluctance to retelling his history. That history would turn a woman away. But he knew Mara. She wouldn't think any less of him. But would she understand why he'd never have children? Would she push him for kids five years down the road, and he'd have to break her heart then?

"Trust your instincts with my daughter. Talk to her." She motioned to the peaches, waiting in the blender. "She inspires you. She came today to support you. Don't lose sight of that because of your past. Or your fear."

The kitchen door swung open. Cathal, a beer in hand, waved his arm. "Fifteen minutes."

Lindsay patted Rian's arm. "Let's cook, honey."

He'd focus on the competition and let his mind simmer on Lindsay's words. He was in love with Mara. Now, if he could only trust that to be enough for her.

"Cathal, take Lindsay to the bar for a bottle of whiskey."

Cathal's eyes lit up. "I will do so happily. Which kind?"

Rian smirked. "You can pick. I'll need it in ninety seconds."

Lindsay left, returning a moment later with one of their most expensive bottles of Jameson. Of course, Cathal would choose that.

The crust of the cobbler cooled on the stove, having been made earlier by Lindsay. He poured the peach puree into a saucepan and then added the brown sugar and Jameson. In another pot, the peaches from earlier simmered in sugar.

Simple.

A dessert that his ma would have loved. And, of course, he never stopped thinking of Mara with the fresh peach scent in the air.

Lindsay whipped the heavy cream in a bowl, handing it to him as he assembled three plates. As a last thought, he did a fourth for Mara. He'd like her to try the dessert that she inspired.

Lindsay took a spoon and tasted the puree. "That is delicious."

"Good." He wiped the edge of the plate, cleaning it, and slid the plates to the other side as Cathal came in.

"Time."

Rian finally glanced at Philip. He'd ignored the other chef for the most part. Philip yelled in his kitchen. Slammed things. Threw things. He was a big version of a three-year-old with a kitchen playset.

Philip crossed his arms, a cocky smile on his face. "May the best man win."

Lindsay set her hand on her hip. "Good. That means you'll lose by default."

The smile slipped from his face.

Rian and Cathal both laughed. Rian hugged Lindsay. "Thank you. For being here. Helping."

"This has been the highlight of my year. I'm grateful you and my daughter found each other. Take some time, Rian." She patted him on the back. "You have some decisions to make. Just know, whatever you and Mara decide to do, you have our support." She pulled away and smiled. "Now, I think I'll go see my daughter."

Cathal took out the food for the blind taste test, leaving the fourth plate for Mara. She'd have to wait until after the judges made their decision.

Philip walked over and held his hand out. "I meant it earlier. May the best dish win."

Rian shook his hand. "If you ever speak to my girlfriend the way you did earlier, I will lay your ass out on the ground." He left Philip standing alone in the kitchen to find Mara.

She stood to the side, between her ma and Selena, watching along with everyone else the decision of the judges.

They were trying his dish. He glanced at them, halfway wondering about their reaction, but his gaze returned to Mara.

She looked at him, didn't smile, and then looked away.

He shoved his hands in his pockets. Damn, he'd screwed up. Her ma had been right, though. He needed to decide.

Then he needed to give her a choice. If she stayed with him, he didn't want kids. That may never change. She didn't need to go into a relationship, thinking it might.

If she walked away—

The judges stood up. He knew them all. So did Philip. They'd mutually agreed on who'd they invite in for the event. Casey hadn't been his first choice. The nineteen-year-old was a prodigy with a big ego.

Virginia held up a card. "We made a decision. It was close. Very close." She looked to the back of the room, where Rian and Philip both stood. "I'm not sure why neither one of you have pushed yourself before today. You both had some genius moments that I will definitely write about in my next article. But one of you accomplished something I had doubted would happen. You created a unique flavor that may be the perfect representation of yourself." She smiled at Rian. "Rian, you're the winner."

The crowd cheered as relief seeped into his body. He wouldn't have to promote the pompous jerk's restaurant, and the after-school center would get additional funds.

Instead of acting like an idiot, Philip shook Rian's hand and quietly left. Rian would make sure he held up his end of the bargain and cut Mara's program a check by the end of the month.

A mass of people surrounded him, shaking his hand, giving him hugs. Brogan pushed through the crowd and give him a massive hug that he returned.

Selena was next. Rian shielded her from the press of people, passing her back to Brogan. Cathal slapped him on the back.

But no Mara.

He looked to where she stood before, and only Lindsay remained.

Lindsay shrugged.

He'd won the competition and possibly lost his heart in the process.

Or maybe he'd found it.

25

For the third day in a row, Mara walked laps around her apartment's kitchen, contemplating whether or not to call Rian, pissing off Dash each time she passed his favorite hiding spot. He'd gotten in two good swipes with his paw. The soft pad didn't do any damage, but even though she expected it each time, it still made her jump.

Last she'd heard, Rian was still in Atlanta. Part of her wondered if he would jet off somewhere, ignoring their issue and ignoring that she even existed. That's how he'd survived before dating her. She recognized it now. Staying in one place was what wrecked him.

But he hadn't left.

The competition brought the restaurant the recognition they'd hoped. Yesterday, she'd seen Cathal being interviewed on a local morning talk show. Even though the host was nearly twenty years older than he was, she wouldn't be surprised if Cathal hadn't talked the woman into having a drink or two that evening based on the chemistry she'd seen on screen.

She held up her phone and then sat it back down on the

table. No. She wouldn't cave first. Rian could make an effort. She wouldn't force herself on him.

Pain and fear snaked through her body. If he never called, then what?

She took a deep breath and walked away from her phone. Her body ached with the realization that her love might be one-sided. How could he stay away if he did love her?

She finished getting dressed and opened her freezer to grab a frozen meal. Chicken Alfredo. She tossed it into her lunch bag.

It would be a good day. Today, Romeo came back to the after-school center. The Board of Trustees took her recommendation for reinstatement. Besides, Mara's argument about the other kid starting the fight and Selena's letter covering Romeo as a great employee over the past few weeks, went a long way.

The knock at her door made her pause. It was a quarter till eight. Her heart immediately hoped Rian had shown up.

But yesterday she'd yanked open the door expecting Rian only to have the FedEx delivery woman back away slowly after getting her signature.

And the day before a Boy Scout selling popcorn door-to-door looked a little nervous when Mara had to wipe away tears while writing a check.

She swallowed, set her lunch bag down, and crossed the room, side-stepping Dash's paw.

"Mara?" Rian's voice called. "Please open up."

Her heart beat twice as fast at the sound of his voice. He'd shown up. She unlocked the door and opened it.

Rian stood there with a cardboard box in his hands. He hadn't worn a black T-shirt as usual, and of all things, that surprised her. It was gray, with a black picture of the Golden

Gate Bridge across his chest. He had circles under his eyes. His hair was unkept. And he basically looked like complete hell.

Her heart seized. "Rian—"

"Don't say anything yet." He shifted the box in his arms. "Can I come in?"

She moved from the doorway. "Of course. What is that?"

He set the box on the table. "We need to talk." He turned toward her. "But I need to do something first."

Mara braced herself for a kiss.

But instead of a kiss, Rian pulled a garbage bag out of the box he'd brought and walked to her freezer. "I was going to bring you flowers."

She wrapped her arms around her stomach, bracing herself for whatever he had to say. Or what he wouldn't say. "I don't want flowers from you, Rian."

"I know." In three seconds, he snatched open the freezer door and tossed every frozen dinner she owned into the black bag.

"What are you doing?" She walked up beside him, wanting to grab the bag away. "You're wasting perfectly good food."

He shook his head. "No. I'm making room for good food." He spotted her lunch box. "Is there one in there?"

She held the bag to her chest. "Yes. I love this Alfredo."

"I hope you enjoy it." He tied the bag and tossed it to the corner of the kitchen. Then, he began to unload black trays of food into her fridge. "I made you fifteen frozen dinners."

She gaped at him. "You made those for me?"

"Yes." He held the last one in his hand. "Do you still want that Alfredo?"

Mara took the offered tray and passed him the boxed lunch. "Hell, no. You really didn't have to do this."

"I had to do something to take my mind off the thought that I've lost you."

"Rian—"

"Mara, I'm sorry." He lifted his eyes to meet hers, leaning back against the refrigerator and crossing his arms. "I realize I should have told you the truth from the first time you asked, but it's not easy to speak about. You'll be the first person, outside of my family, that knows about my child."

Every instinct in her wanted to shield him from going through the pain of retelling it. But he needed to. He needed to know he could talk to her about it. He could fall apart with her. She'd help put him back together again.

He closed his eyes. "At nineteen, my girlfriend became pregnant. We married." He blew out a heavy breath. "My little girl didn't make it but a few hours after she was born." He opened his eyes. The pain reflected there brought her to tears again. "I didn't lie to you. I might have misspoken on purpose, but I couldn't have any more children. I won't survive if something were to happen a second time."

He shoved his hands in his pockets. "And discussing it won't change anything, Mara." His blue eyes watched her. "I do not want children. I should have walked away from you a long time ago before things got this serious. I know you want to be a mother. You'd make an amazing one. I see how you are with all the kids."

"Besides this, besides your worry over my desire for kids, do you want to walk away? Leave? Never see me again?"

"No." He sighed. "I know I should. You want more than I can give you. Knowing that, not being enough for you, will destroy me just the same."

"Rian, you are what I want." She held her hands out. "I love you."

Saying the words didn't frighten her. She meant them. She loved Rian.

He pushed away from the refrigerator as she stepped closer. "You do?"

"Yes."

He gently gripped her upper arms, bringing their bodies together. "Are you saying you're willing to stay with me?"

The man still didn't get it. "I love you. Did you not hear me?" She smirked. "That means that I want to be with you."

"But kids—" His hands slipped from her shoulders to cup her face.

She held onto his wrists. He might change his mind about kids. He might not. As long as he was there, she was happy.

"Just don't shut me out. I can't stand that. Talk to me. The truth. Deciding if we want kids is a pretty far way down the road, anyway. If we get to that point, then we'll talk about it and make a decision. Together. And if you still don't want them, I'm not going anywhere."

His lips tilted up on one side, not quite a smile, but it broke through the intensity of his gaze. He leaned down and kissed her. "Amara, I love you, and I have no idea what the hell to do about it."

Her entire body relaxed against his. He loved her.

That was enough.

"Well," she began, wrapping her arms around his neck. "Making me frozen dinners is a start."

"You know—" he nipped at her bottom lip, "—if you move in with me, I won't have to make those for you."

"Move in." Nothing but excitement hummed through her. "Can I decorate? You know, add a colorful rug to the kitchen or something? Maybe a bright blue hand towel in the bathroom."

He laughed and hugged her. "Absolutely."

She glanced down at Dash. He'd crawled out of his hiding spot underneath the chair in the entryway. His tail swished. "You're not allergic to cats, are you?"

"I want you there with me. I don't care who you bring or what you do to the condo." He surveyed her apartment, the messy, cluttered place that she'd happily give up for him. "So, this is where you live?"

She tugged his head down, kissing him hard on the mouth. "Not any longer."

EPILOGUE

O'Keeley's was slammed. Standing room only at the bar. The loud band played from their small stage in the corner. Every table was full. Extra waitstaff rushed around for the Saturday night.

And Cathal was in charge of it all.

He'd insisted that Brogan keep Selena at home to rest. His niece, Rosie, didn't need to make an early appearance. And with Rian in Greece with Mara, that left the youngest O'Keeley to run the show. He could. He had a law degree from Georgetown. The running of the restaurant wasn't his issue.

It threw a kink into his weekly plans. One he looked forward to. He'd missed going to Fiona's last night, and it looked like he might miss tonight as well.

Damn shame. He wanted nothing more than to sit at the end of her bar with a glass of whiskey and try to charm a smile from his pretty bartender. It was hard work, too. Fiona was made of steel and could slice a man in half with her fairy eyes.

"Excuse me? Do you work here?" A burly man with a

chest-length beard tapped him on the shoulder.

Cathal buttoned his suit jacket as he turned. "Yes. How can I help you today, sir?"

The guy hitched his thumb over his shoulder. "The men's restroom is out of toilet paper, and the last stall is clogged."

These must be the executive duties that Brogan mentioned. Cathal walked away toward the supply closet. He'd much rather be with Fiona. But, seeing as her bar would shortly be closed after he turned the lights out in O'Keeley's, he'd have to settle for a glass of his own whiskey at his apartment. After working the past two days and exhausting himself, he might actually get a few hours of sleep.

He walked out of the men's restroom as Rachel, Mara's friend, walked out of the women's. Her dress was red, tight, and short, revealing miles of long legs.

"Well, hey there, stranger," she said, with a full, sexy smile. "I assumed you might be running the show."

"I'm the responsible brother. Didn't you know that." He grinned at her, remembering their one, brief date. It wasn't exactly a date. More like a couple of drinks, kissing, and dropping her off at her place, alone. He had no intention of messing up Rian's chance with Mara at the time.

"I bet you're lonely with everyone out of town." She stopped by the stairs the led up to their upper dining room.

The statement was meant as a joke, but it hit a little too close to home. Even with a woman, he sometimes felt lonely. But he liked Rachel.

"I can keep you company."

He leaned on the banister. "I'm afraid I won't be able to leave until after the pub closes down. Could be one in the morning at the rate we're going."

"I might just be up to going out then."

He tilted his head to the side, watching her a long moment until she shifted toward him. He liked reading signals from women. They were like a green light to take another step and another until they both ended up with what they wanted, be it drinks and a handshake or more.

"I was thinking of staying in."

"My place?" she asked.

Her lack of hesitation was another sign they were on the same page. "Absolutely." As a rule, he didn't bring women back to his place. He always thought of his apartment as messy. Rian called it a health hazard. And he didn't need the memories.

"Do you still have my number?"

He pulled out his phone. "Rachel V."

She laughed. "How many Rachels do you have on your phone?"

Six. But he wouldn't tell her that. "You're the only Rachel I'm calling tonight."

"So, I'll see you about one or one-thirty?"

He scratched his cheek, thinking of only one other woman. "Let's say two. I have someone I need to swing by and see for a few minutes."

Rachel smirked. "Another woman?"

"Yes. But she doesn't find me nearly as appealing."

"Her loss, my gain." She turned and walked up the stairs. He watched her go, glad to have the company later. It'd keep his mind off his past.

And he'd sleep. It wouldn't be for long, and he'd leave early in the morning, but a few hours of mindless sleep were worth it.

The End

ABOUT THE AUTHOR

Palmer Jones writes fun and flirty, romantic fiction. Born and raised in the South, she loves to travel but will always call Georgia her home. With a degree in accounting, she spends part of her day immersed in numbers. The rest of the time is spent with her friends, family, and hiding away in the worlds she creates through her stories.

f

ACKNOWLEDGMENTS

I want to thank several people that helped with not only writing this book but also supporting me in so many ways. My husband, my parents, and my friends for listening to all my ramblings and reading my work.

Thank you to Jessie, for sticking with me throughout my crazy writing journey. Thank you Kim for being so supportive.

I'd also like to thank a few individuals who helped make this a great book. JD&J Design for the beautiful cover. Patricia Ogilvie for helping put the final touches on the book.

Made in the USA
Middletown, DE
15 September 2020

19907569R00142